DEDICATION

To my mom, who always read to me when I was young, and kindled my love of books.

CONTENTS

Chapter 1	Pancakes for Breakfast	1
Chapter 2	The Globe of Tarahabi	11
Chapter 3	A Voyage by Train	24
Chapter 4	Welcome To Jesburgon	35
Chapter 5	The Whisp	48
Chapter 6	The Mirror	63
Chapter 7	The Deal	83
Chapter 8	Threat	96
Chapter 9	Hope Is Lost	106
Chapter 10	The Importance of Friendship	116
Chapter 11	Into the Dragon's Lair	124
Chapter 12	Fate	134
Chapter 13	Elemental Power	141
Chapter 14	Alyk	153
Epilogue		161
About the Author		166

CHAPTER 1

PANCAKES FOR BREAKFAST

The day my life changed forever, I woke up to my sister Oranah screaming into my ear.

"Wake up, Lexa! You're going to be late! Mum's already made breakfast."

I groaned and rolled onto my stomach. Why would I care if I were late for school? Every day was the same in my boring little village.

"*Umph!*" Something soft but firm slammed into the back of my head, knocking the breath out of me. I rolled back around to face Oranah with half-closed, tired eyes. She stood beside my small bed smirking, with a pillow raised in her hands. "Will you stop doing that?" I asked, irritated by my sister's childish behaviour.

At eleven years old and two years younger than me, Oranah was still a child. But did that really mean she had to act like it all the time?

I sighed, and started to roll over again. Before I could fall back into a peaceful sleep, however, Oranah decided to try a new tactic.

"There are pancakes on the table!" Oranah said in a singsong voice.

Pancakes?

I sat up, suddenly wide awake. My sister snickered. She tossed her pillow back onto her unmade bed beside mine and raced back downstairs, her dirty blonde hair flying behind her.

I slid my legs over the side of my bed and went over to the closet. My dad's clothes were on the top shelf, my mother's on the next shelf down. My clothes were on the third shelf from the top and Oranah's on the bottom. My whole family shared a bedroom. We had to, since there were only three rooms in our tiny house. The bedroom was upstairs, while the kitchen and bathroom were located on the first floor. It was small, but that minor detail didn't matter; the main thing was that we were happy. Well, more or less happy.

I reached onto my shelf and picked out the first dress my hands brushed against. It happened to be the dull brown one I had worn when a few of my friends and I had played in a field on the farm of my best friend Mira's aunt and uncle. I had tripped over Brigelle's boot and had gotten grass stains all over the front of my dress when I had fallen. As I slipped the dress over my head, I noticed that the stains were still there.

I'll wash them off after breakfast, I thought. Speaking of which …

The scent of fresh pancakes entered my nose as I walked down the stairs to the kitchen. My mother never made pancakes unless it was a special occasion. Confused, I walked over to the four-seat table where my father and Oranah were already sitting. My mother was attempting to flip pancakes with a big wooden spoon. She was standing by the small stove with her back to me. I sat down at the table next to my little sister, who was already finishing her pancakes.

"What's the occasion?" I asked casually.

My family stopped what they were doing to stare at me. Oranah's mouth was open. She had just been about to stuff another pancake into her mouth but had stopped halfway there. The pancake that should have been in her mouth was back on her plate because she had dropped it.

My father had been jotting something down in a leather notebook for his job. By the looks of it, he'd stopped mid sentence, his pen still clutched in his hand. My mother had turned around to face me. She had an odd expression on her face, as if she were angry, but confused and surprised at the same time. She was holding her wooden spoon in her hand, a newly made pancake balancing on the top. It was wobbling, on the verge of falling off.

My family just stared at me for a few seconds. It felt like someone had pressed a pause button on my life, although I knew no one had, because I could hear the other pancakes still sizzling behind my mother.

Finally, my mother spoke, slowly shaking her head. "How could you have forgotten?"

Forgotten what? Oh, *no*. I couldn't have.

"It's your Talent Gaining day."

As soon as she said those words I felt extremely stupid. Of course! What other reason could there be to celebrate? I, like all the other children at school, had been dreaming about my Talent Gaining ever since I was very young. *How* could I have forgotten?

The Talent Gaining was a special ceremony held every year on the first of May, for all children who'd turned thirteen since the previous Talent Gaining. At exactly eleven o'clock in the morning, the village Seer would bring out the globe of Tarahabi, and one by one the children would stand in front of the globe to gain their talent. You could have the power to turn invisible, or the power to fly. You might be telepathic, or telekinetic. There was a huge variety of options. But there *was* a catch. There was the rare possibility of having *no* talent whatsoever. In that case, you were exiled from Mencia.

A rush of excitement swept through me. Today was the day I had been waiting for my whole life. Today, I would discover my talent ... and I definitely couldn't wear my grass-stained brown dress.

I raced back upstairs and over to the closet. I hummed to myself as I rummaged around my shelf to find the dress I had in mind. I found it at the very back, squashed up against the wall, because I seldom wore it.

I pulled the dress out and held it up so I could look at it. It was really pretty. Made from a soft, silky blue material, it was different from my other, more casual dresses. I grinned as I took off my brown dress and slipped the blue one over my head. The skirt ended just below my knees and the sleeves didn't leave my shoulders so I hoped it was not too chilly outside.

I twirled and I watched the blue skirt floating around me, rippling like water. Looking up, a pearly white colour from my mother's shelf caught my attention.

My mother hardly ever used her special hair comb — only on days of celebration or important work occasions. *I'd* only ever used it twice — once when my friend Aleine's brother got married and once when my school class went on a day trip to Mencia's main village. To be fair, I was not technically even *allowed* to use the comb. But today was my Talent Gaining — I had to look my best. And anyway, I was the only one upstairs. No one would notice if I just …

I reached up and snatched the comb off

my mother's shelf. I took a few seconds to admire it before combing through my wavy, chocolate brown hair. The comb was pearl white with a hint of pink. The sparkling gems along the handle glistened as I tilted it this way and that to catch the light. My mother used to tell me stories about how she had gotten her comb from a mermaid – stories that I now laugh at myself for believing.

Doing something I knew I wasn't allowed to had sharpened my senses, so I jumped when I heard the creek of the bottom stair.

Panicking, I pulled the comb out of my hair. I then rushed over to the closet and shoved the comb back into its spot on the edge of the shelf, just as my father poked his head into the room.

"Hurry up Lexa! You're going to be late if you don't eat your pancakes now! Oranah's already left!"

Oranah had already left? I must have woken up later than I realized. Even so, I still was not in much of a hurry. My class had no lessons today, so we didn't have to be at school for nine like the rest of the children in the village. Instead, we had to arrive at ten, in order to be ready for the

Talent Gaining at eleven.

I followed my father downstairs and sat down at the table – again – where my pancakes were already cooling. They were not my mother's best – tiny, and an odd brownish color – but they tasted all right. I gobbled them quickly, and then brought my empty plate over to the sink, where my mother was washing dirty dishes. I placed my plate in the soapy water, then reached up on my toes and gave my mother a quick peck on the cheek.

"Wish me luck!" I said. I turned and started towards the door.

"Wait Lexa!" My mother stopped me. I turned back around, just a few steps from the door.

My mother was in no hurry; she carefully untied her apron and lifted the strap over her head. She took something out of the front pocket of the apron before hanging it on the closest chair. Finally, she came over to me, her right hand closed tightly around the thing she had taken from her pocket. She held out her hand to reveal a beautiful necklace.

I gasped softly at the sight of the extraordinary pendant – a magnificent ocean blue jewel shaped like a teardrop. I couldn't take my eyes off of it. It was the most enchanting thing I'd ever seen.

"My mother gave this to me on my Talent Gaining," she told me, as she lifted the silver chain over my head to rest around my neck. I gazed into the captivating blue jewel. "And now ... I'm giving it to you."

My eyes stung. I'd never been so happy. I'd never felt so much love towards my mother.

Love. My heart exploded with it.

I looked up at my mother, into her deep blue eyes, and the memory came rushing back to me.

I was young – maybe four or five – when my grandmother died. I had never been close to my mother's mother, as she had lived in a different village, and I had hardly ever seen her. But she and my mother had been very close indeed, perhaps because my mother was an only child. She didn't have any sisters or brothers to talk to while she was growing up.

I had stood next to my mother at the funeral, and held her hand. I now remembered looking up at her face and feeling like someone had spilt a bucket of ice water over my head.

I had never seen my mother – or any

adult for that matter – look so sad, and it had come as a real shock.

I remembered watching my mother look down at her chest where her necklace sat. She had then picked up the aqua blue jewel with her thumb and forefinger and stared into it, lost in thought. The jewel was the same deep-sea blue colour as her eyes.

A single tear had trickled down her cheek.

Not wanting to look any longer, I had finally wrapped my small arms around my mother's legs and buried my face into them. After a few seconds, I had felt fingers run through my hair, and warm arms had wrapped around me. I had looked up into my mother's glistening eyes, now fixed on me. She had then crouched down, so that we were the same height, and continued to gaze at me for a few more seconds. Then she had pulled me into her chest and squeezed me in a tight embrace, before lightly kissing my forehead the way only a mother can.

"Everything will be alright." Her warm breath had caressed my ear as she whispered the words of comfort to me.

Everything will be all right. The words now echoed inside my head as I came back to the present, still staring into my mother's loving blue eyes.

Love and joy burst out of me as I threw my arms around my mother and embraced her.

Everything will be all right. My mother was there for me. Nothing could go wrong if she was there to protect me.

Everything will be all right. I felt safe in her arms. I hoped she would never let me go.

Everything will be all right. I closed my eyes.

"I love you, mum." I whispered.

I felt my mother's soft lips against my forehead as she kissed me, the way only a mother can.

Everything would be all right.

CHAPTER 2

THE GLOBE OF TARAHABI

Not even the bad weather could bring my spirits down. The sky was gray and cloudy. It was cold and a bit windy, and it had rained the night before. The rain had collected in large puddles that were scattered everywhere. The dirt road was now a mud road.

The miserable day had kept everyone inside, so no one was there to greet me, or to wish me luck, but the smile my mother had given me was still glued to my face.

I'm sure I looked stupid wearing my big smile and fancy dress, as I skipped down the mud road towards my school, but that didn't matter to me. I came to a puddle on the side of the road that was clear enough for me to see my reflection in it. If I say so myself, I thought I looked rather beautiful. My hair was straighter than usual, and my dress flattered my skin, but the thing that stood out was my new necklace. My eyes were a slightly different shade of blue from it – unlike my mother's – but it still sparkled like a midnight star. The jewel, I now realized, was the same color as the ocean. It looked like a drop of water about to fall from the silver chain around my neck. It really was something.

Suddenly, I felt a hand on my shoulder. I gasped in surprise and turned around, expecting to see Mira, my best friend from school. Instead of Mira's smiling young face, however, I saw an old one, with dark brown eyes, curly gray hair and wrinkles. Bya was the oldest and wisest member of our village. She was the village Seer, the one with the rare talent of seeing into the future. Bya's eyes were normally small and friendly, but today they were wide open and full of fear. It was for this reason that my smile did not return to my face when I saw her.

Bya wasted no time in telling me what was on her mind, pausing to take deep breaths after every few words, as if she'd just run the length of our village.

"Miss Foote! ... " *breath* " ... I have seen that ... " *breath* " ... you are in great danger! ... " *breath* ... *breath* " ... you must beware! ... " *breath* "... the enemies are stronger together." Then she stared into my eyes, hoping for a sign that I had understood. She did not find it, because I had been confused ever since she had placed her hand on my shoulder. That was the thing with Bya. The poor woman tried to tell us about danger, or good fortune, but no one ever seemed to understand. If the village didn't love her so much, we probably would have asked King Trub, the ruler of Mencia, for a different Seer.

After a few seconds, Bya gave up trying to make me understand. She sighed and stared into space, lost in thought. I wasn't sure if I should continue on my way. Before I could decide, Bya looked back at me. She seemed to be surprised that I was still there.

"Well, go on then," she said.

I decided to walk the rest of the way to my school. All the cheerfulness had drained from my body, replaced with anger at not being able to understand Bya's prediction, as well as worries, for she had told me I was in danger – from what? – and confusion, for nothing that had just happened made any sense. I now felt miserable.

I started kicking around a rock that I found on the road. It gave me something to look at; something to do until I eventually got to school. My school was one of the oldest buildings in my village. It was made out of bricks that had turned brown and started crumbling over the years. Some people said that it had been built even before the Great War of Laze - which had happened more than two hundred years ago. I went inside and found my classmates standing around in the front entrance. All the other children seemed to be already in class. Was I really that late? I glanced up at the tiny clock above the double doors leading outside. Ten o'clock, it read. Nope, I was right on time. Then my stomach dropped when I remembered that the clock was seven minutes behind.

When Mira realized I was there she hurried over to me.

"Lexa! Why are you so late? We've been waiting for you for like, a thousand years!" Mira was loud, talkative, and always happy. She had bright orange hair and blue eyes. You could see her dimples when she smiled, which was pretty much all the time. Mira was Little Miss Sunshine inside and out. Everyone looked up when they heard Mira's voice, and suddenly I was the center of attention, but the boys and girls swarming around me were not as smiley as a Little Miss Sunshine.

"You're so late!"

"What took you so long?"

"Now we might be late for the Talent Gaining, and it's all your fault!"

"Mrs. Roy! Lexa's finally here!"

Our teacher, Mrs. Roy, came over to me. Mrs. Roy was a tall woman with straight blonde hair that she had arranged neatly in a tight bun on top of her head. She never seemed to be very happy and – perhaps because of her height – thought that she was better than everyone around her. As Mrs. Roy slowly walked towards me, the kids around me parted to clear a path for her. She stopped about two feet from my face and put her hands on her hips, looking down at me with disgust.

"You're late," she told me. I very much wanted to say, "So I've been told," but I had tried that sort of thing with Mrs. Roy before, and it had not ended well. Instead, I just nodded, looking up at her with what I hoped were big, scared, innocent eyes. That was the tactic that worked best with Mrs. Roy. Make her feel big and intimidating and you wouldn't get much of a punishment.

The tactic worked. I saw her eyes move from mine, to my clothes. She nodded. "Nice appropriate dress. Good," she said. Then she turned and walked down the hall. My classmates and I glanced at one another before following her into a classroom.

It was not our usual classroom, but rather one that served as a backstage area for the auditorium. The walls were a funny yellow color, and the paint was peeling off. On the left side of the classroom was a chalkboard; small, yet just big enough to write a sentence that could be read from the other side of the room. There were ten desks, which fit my class perfectly as there were ten of us. In the back of the room there was a door that led to the ridiculously tiny stage in the auditorium. That itty-bitty stage would be where we would get our talents.

When Mrs. Roy reached the front, she turned around to face the desks like she taught in that classroom every day. Then she looked at us, and raised her eyebrows expectantly. All at once, we stopped looking around at this new room and hurried to find a seat. I was one of the last to sit down, so I found myself in the front row next to Mira. It seemed that we were two of the only ones who didn't fear Mrs. Roy. No one said a word as we sat down, but I'm sure Mira had to bite her tongue. When Mrs. Roy was satisfied that everyone was silent, she began to give us the well-rehearsed speech that she gave her class every year before their Talent Gaining.

"Almost two hundred and fifty years ago," she began, "there lived an old miner by the name of Tarahabi. His family was poor and lived off of only what Tarahabi would find down in the mines. And so when the rumours spread that there was gold hiding in a nearby mineshaft, Tarahabi was of the first to go looking for it. However, the old miner did not find his gold; he found something much better and far more valuable. A large, beautiful crystal.

"The crystal was no ordinary stone, as Tarahabi soon found out," Mrs. Roy continued. "As he stared into it, the gem turned a delicate shade of baby blue, and then his hand seemingly dissolved into thin air, so that the crystal seemed to be floating. Soon his whole body had disappeared, and it gradually dawned on him that the crystal had given him the power to turn invisible.

"Tarahabi knew he could not let the crystal's powers go to waste, and so he took his discovery to his king, who rewarded Tarahabi with enough gold to last him for the rest of his life. The king named the crystal *the Globe of Tarahabi* after its finder.

"It wasn't long before the king discovered that the crystal not only had the power to make one invisible, but that it bestowed different powers on different people. Since he cared much for his people, he decided that everyone should benefit and immediately set about presenting each and every one with a 'talent' as he called them. Not far into his quest to make his people happy, the king discovered that no child under the age of thirteen could be presented with a talent. However, that problem was easily solved. Every year on the first of May, there would be a Talent Gaining for each village and all the children who'd turned thirteen since the previous Talent Gaining would attend.

"For years, this went on, until around fifty years later something went wrong. Sometimes the Globe of Tarahabi would not present an individual with a talent. Instead, it would proclaim them as 'untalented'. This was rare, but could not be ignored, for soon the untalented began to blame the talented of stealing the talents that were rightfully theirs. A war broke out between the talented and the untalented. The Great War of Laze."

Mrs. Roy paused at this stage, as if to show

respect for that momentous event. She then closed her eyes briefly before continuing.

"It was a terrible time. Many innocent people were killed, untalented and talented alike. Then, finally, the king was murdered by an untalented, causing the entire country to dissolve into chaos.

"Finally, the new king did the only thing he could think of," Mrs. Roy said. "He sent the untalented away, to a mysterious place where no one would ever find them. We have not heard from the untalented since."

I had so many questions. Some, I'm sure, were questions that everyone was asking themselves, such as, "Where do the untalented go?" and "Why have we never heard from them?" In addition to these questions, I was also wondering to myself, "How in the world did Mrs. Roy memorize all that?" I felt like I was wandering through a tunnel of blackness. I could spot no clues, but a voice inside my head did tell me that she probably hadn't actually *memorized* the entire story. She was more likely just telling it in her own words, in the right order.

Mrs. Roy was quiet for a few minutes, probably allowing what she had said to sink in before continuing.

"It's almost time," she then said. "When I

call your name, go line up by the stage door." Her words snapped us out of our daze and we got excited all over again. A ball of excitement mixed with nervousness exploded somewhere in my stomach and rushed to the rest of my body. My hands began to get sweaty. Mrs. Roy took out a piece of paper on which our names were listed in alphabetical order, according to our surnames. I don't know why she needed it. All of our other teachers had memorized our order by May. She read the first name.

"Haron Bent."

Haron got up from his seat at the back of the room and shuffled his way over to the door. I felt bad for him. Haron was very shy. He hated being first or the center of attention – unlike Mira. It didn't make things any easier for him that he was the tallest in the class.

"Naja Ellens."

Naja was the smartest girl in our class – she aced every test and seemed to understand everything perfectly – but not even close to the prettiest. Naja got up from her seat behind me and went over to stand next to Haron.

"Lexa Foote."

Me. I stood up and confidently walked over to stand behind Naja. After me came Aluji Kerr, then Mira Lotson, who skipped over to her place in line when her name was called, Mrs. Roy's glare following her. Eventually, everyone was in line. Now we were just waiting for Bya to come with the Globe of Tarahabi, then we would begin.

I could hear all of our families in the next room, chatting away. They seemed almost as excited as I felt. I wondered why. It was *our* Talent Gaining after all.

Quickly, everything went silent, so I knew Bya had just walked into the room. My heart sped up a little. This was it.

Mrs. Roy opened the door and gestured for Haron to go inside. He was shaking all over. He closed his eyes and took a deep breath. Mrs. Roy was losing the tiny bit of patience that she had in life. She cleared her throat, and Haron's eyes snapped open. Mrs. Roy raised her eyebrows at him, then he stepped out onto the little stage and Mrs. Roy closed the door.

It took a lot less time than I expected. He'd only been in there for about a minute when I heard some polite applause and he came back out. A smile of happiness and relief was on his face. Mrs. Roy ordered him to sit down at a desk, and he obeyed. Then it was Naja's turn to go in.

Now I was really starting to get nervous.

My hands were sticky with sweat and I was breathing heavily. A part of me never wanted Naja to come out, but she did, with a similar smile to Haron's on her face.

Then Mrs. Roy was telling me to go in. It was my turn. I took a deep breath and walked out onto the stage. The auditorium wasn't as big as one would expect. It was the same size as the room I had just come out of. The stage was just big enough for me, Bya, and the table on which the Globe of Tarahabi sat. There were about thirty people watching me. I spotted my family in the far left corner. I looked into my mother's proud face for courage, and then I turned to Bya. The Seer looked almost as scared as she'd appeared earlier, and hesitated before saying, "Stare into the Globe of Tarahabi, and it will help you discover the talent hidden deep within you." She whispered so no one else would hear.

My gaze shifted from her to the globe. It was extremely beautiful. It looked as if it had once been a sphere, but there were chunks missing from it.

I stared into it. I could tell I'd been staring for longer than Haron or Naja, because I heard people starting to shift awkwardly in their seats. Then something happened. At first, it looked like a tiny ball of red gas that formed in the center of the globe. It grew bigger and bigger until it filled the entire globe. There was a collective gasp of fear from the audience. One thing was for certain, this had not happened with Haron or Naja. Then suddenly, my blood went cold as I finally figured out what it meant.

I had no talent.

CHAPTER 3

A VOYAGE BY TRAIN

I was stunned. I couldn't move. Tears welled up in my eyes and my breathing became unsteady. Many thoughts and emotions were swimming around in my head. This was not what I had expected.

I had wondered my whole life up until then what my talent would be. But I didn't have one. I was untalented.

I felt as if my insides had fallen off a cliff and left my body behind as I realized ... I was going to be taken away. I would never get to finish my life with the people in my little village that I'd grown up knowing. Mira,

Oranah, Mrs. Roy, Bya, my mother ... I would never see any of them again.

I felt a hand on my arm and I came back to reality. It was one of the guards from the main village of Mencia – a guard was sent to watch over the Talent Gaining in every village. He transported the Globe of Tarahabi from village to village and collected the untalented. The people like me.

The guard led me through the crowd towards the door. The audience parted to make a path for us. We were walking fast. I turned around to look at Bya, who looked back at me helplessly. With a jolt I realized that this was what she had tried to warn me about. The tears in my eyes finally poured down my cheeks.

I must have been walking slower because I tripped, but the guard kept a firm grip on my arm. Just before we reached the door, I looked back at my mother. Her ocean blue eyes sparkled with tears. I wanted to run over and let her squeeze me in a tight hug. I wanted her to tell me that everything would be fine – just like she always did – then all my worries and troubles would disappear. But now things were different. Now that I was untalented, that wouldn't happen anymore. I managed to make eye contact for only a second before the guard pulled me out the door.

I could only hear the teachers closing their classroom doors so their classes wouldn't be distracted by me, as tears blurred my vision. Nobody cared about me. Not anymore. Now that I was untalented, they wanted me to get out of their lives. I cried harder.

The next five minutes were quite possibly the most miserable of my life. I could hardly see where we were going because of my teary eyes. I was lost in my own horrible thoughts. It was like falling down a long black hole. I couldn't see the bottom but I knew that soon I would reach it. A kind of death awaited me.

When my sobbing decreased enough to allow me to take in my surroundings, I saw that we were nearing the train station. I walked a bit faster, and less carelessly so that the guard was no longer dragging me along. He simply held onto my arm while hurrying along beside me. I could tell the guard was trying not to look at me. It was his job; to take children away from everything they loved and send them away to who knows where. It was the only way for him to earn money. But why should he care? He should be glad, for he wasn't the one being sent away. He wasn't untalented, like me.

At first, I was confused when we passed the ticket booth without stopping, but of course you couldn't just buy a ticket to the place I was going.

We walked all the way to the very last track. In all my life I'd never seen a train there. But, today, my eyes were met by the smallest train that I'd ever seen. It consisted of just two compartments that looked like big boxes on wheels. I wondered where I was supposed to sit. As we got closer, I saw a door on the side of each box, but there were no windows.

The guard spoke to me. "You're lucky," he said. "There are a few of you this time, so you won't be alone, at least." I was surprised. It was rare to be untalented, and I hadn't expected anyone else to join me on the journey to wherever it was I was going.

We reached the small train and the guard led me over to the door of the second compartment. He slid open the door. There was no light inside other than the faint sunlight coming in through the doorway, but I could still just about see four people sitting along the sides – two girls and two boys. Judging by what the guard had said, there were more of us than he had expected, but I was too depressed to wonder why.

The guard released his grip on my arm.

"Go on," he said and nodded towards the inside of the box. I sighed, and stepped into the box with the other children, who looked up at me with empathy. The left corner closest to the door was unoccupied, so I went over and sat down. Then the guard slid the door shut and everything went black.

My eyes were just adjusting to the dark when someone spoke from across the box.

"Welcome aboard." It was a boy. He didn't seem very excited at all, sarcastic, actually.

"Thanks," I said, but I was only being polite.

I could now make out the other kids sitting around. The boy who had spoken had messy dark hair, but I couldn't make out its exact colour. The girl sitting next to me had shoulder length blond hair and pale blue eyes. I imagined she looked pretty in the sunlight, and I couldn't help but feel a hint of jealously. The other girl sat next to the boy who'd spoken. I could tell that she was tall without needing her to stand up. Her legs were stretched out in front of her and even so, the boy's head only came up to her nose. This girl had pencil straight, hazel brown hair that she'd draped over her shoulders and came all the way down to her bellybutton. There was one more boy sitting alone on the side opposite the door. He also had dark hair, except his was shorter, and straight. He sat with his knees pulled up to his chest and his arms around them, so I figured he was still very upset about being taken away.

"Why aren't we moving?" I wondered out loud.

"This happens at every stop," said the blond girl beside me. "My guess is they have to wait until each Talent Gaining is finished. I suspect this train also transports the Globe of Tarahabi from village to village. That must be what the other compartment is for."

I'd never really thought about how the globe of Tarahabi got to each village in time for each Talent Gaining, and the more I thought about what the girl had said, the more I was sure she was right.

"That makes sense," I finally managed to say.

"Well, I've had a lot of time to think about it. I was the first one on the train. By the way, my name is Lae."

I smirked briefly.

"What?" She asked.

"That rhymes" I told her. "By the *way*, my name is … never mind." The tiny bit of fun I'd felt melted away. Lae obviously wasn't a jokey kind of person.

"But my name isn't ... *oh*." Her lips formed an O shape. "Whatever. What's your name anyway?"

" Lexa," I told her sadly.

"Nice to meet you, Lexa." It wasn't Lae who'd spoken. It was the tall girl. "My name is Nika,"

"Mine's Rennoc," said the boy with the messy dark hair beside her.

"I'm Alyk," said the second boy shyly. The others turned to look at him, surprised to hear him speak.

"So you can speak," said Rennoc.

Alyk looked at his feet. "Yes." And that put an end to our awkward conversation.

We sat in silence for a while after that. Then finally, I heard the sound of footsteps approaching from outside. I sat up straight, eagerly waiting for something to happen. I heard the door to the compartment next door slide open, then a muffled thump, and then it slid closed again. The train lurched, then slowly began chugging forwards, gaining speed as it went. I was leaving my village for the last time. I brought my knees up to my chest and sat with arms wrapped around them, my nose tucked in between.

The majority of the ride was passed in silence. From my position in the corner, I watched Nika absentmindedly finger a small chain around her neck. I wondered how much longer we would have to wait until we reached our unknown destination. I wasn't sure if I ever wanted to, but I wouldn't mind a bit of information.

Turning to Lae, I asked, "you said you were the first one on?" She nodded. "Do you know how many stops are left?"

Lae replied almost immediately. "I'm not entirely sure. We've already made seven stops, including mine, but there could have been one or two stops before that."

"Right," I said. There were nine villages in total; eight little ones, and one big one – Mencia's main village – where King Trub's castle was located.

The train was the perfect place to take a nap. It was dark in the box, and the vibrations of the train were soothing, but I couldn't sleep. When I closed my eyes, all I could see was my mother's face. But not her usual warm smile, this was an exact replica of the one of sadness and horror I'd seen just before the guard pulled me out the door.

A bit later, the train screeched to a stop in another station. There were more footsteps, and I heard someone slide open the door of the first compartment again. I heard it slam shut a minute later.

"I think you're right about the globe of Tarahabi, Lae," said Nika.

Lae nodded. "I know."

"It doesn't make sense that they're sending us away," said Rennoc.

"Just because we're untalented," put in Alyk, who sounded close to tears.

"Actually it does make sense," said Lae.

The boys stared at her. "Have you lost your mind?" asked Rennoc.

"No, I'm using it more than you are."

Rennoc scowled.

"Didn't your teacher tell you about how the Talent Gaining started?" She rolled her eyes. "The untalented started the Great War of Laze, so in the end the king sent the untalented away."

I had to agree with her. It did make sense, though I didn't like it. The others must have been thinking the same thing because no one said anything to prove Lae wrong.

We waited in silence for a long time. I knew everyone was wondering the same thing as I was. Would there be someone untalented here?

Suddenly, something started to vibrate on my chest. Only a little bit, but enough for me to feel. I looked down and saw the necklace my mother had given me. Emotions clouded my thoughts while tears clouded my vision once more. The necklace was the last thing my mother had given me. She would never give me anything ever again, and I would never give her anything ever again. I would never get to *see* her ever again. I was alone in the world.

I was so lost in these thoughts that, at first, I didn't notice my necklace's vibrations getting bigger and bigger. I only realised when my chest began to hurt. Alarmed, I quickly covered it with my hands to stop the others from noticing it. That worked for about ten seconds, then it started glowing. My necklace was *creating light* – and it was brightening by the second, shining through my fingers. I looked around franticly to see who had noticed, but the others were oblivious to my strange problem. They were only paying attention to themselves. Like me, they were all holding something to their chests – something *glowing*. I could see the bright light through their fingers. I hadn't noticed that they were wearing necklaces before – with the exception of Nika, though I hadn't thought much of her necklace before. Now that I looked closer, I could see the chains hanging around their necks. Could it be a coincidence that we all had one?

I heard movement outside the door, and it opened. Sunlight poured into the box and I had to squint to see the three people standing there. The guard, a boy with tears still on his cheeks, and a woman. None of them smiled. The woman looked like she was about to burst into tears, but she didn't. Instead she put her hand on the boy's back and led him over to the box. He got in silently, without looking at the rest of us, and went to sit on the floor next to Alyk.

My necklace was buzzing like crazy now. I tucked it inside my dress so that the guard wouldn't see it. Out of the corner of my eye, I saw the others do the same.

The woman looked around inside the box. Her eyes landed on each of us in turn. They widened farther with each person she looked at. Her jaw dropped open. Without warning, she started rapidly speaking in the old language that only Seers studied. Obviously, I was not a Seer, so I couldn't understand the language, but even if I could speak it, I still doubt I would have been able to understand her, she was speaking so fast. Then, the woman turned and sprinted away from the train. The guard eyed us suspiciously before closing the door.

CHAPTER 4

WELCOME TO JESBURGON

By the time the guard's footsteps faded away, my necklace was shaking so much it was hurting my skin. I reached down through the collar of my dress to pick it up.

"What's going on?" someone said, sounding scared. I didn't recognize the voice, so it must have been the new boy. Once again, I could barely see in the darkness of the box. I looked up to tell him that I had no clue when I noticed that he had a glowing necklace draped around his neck as well. That was when I really started to doubt this was all coincidental.

Beside me, Lae was staring at a small spot on the floor, her face scrunched up in concentration. Perhaps she was searching her brain for answers. Lae found a reason for everything, it seemed, so I trusted her to do all the major thinking. I slid over towards her, and my necklace seemed to do the same. The beautiful blue jewel sort of jumped off my chest toward Lae, and Lae's necklace reached out toward mine so both necklaces were vibrating in midair. Lae looked up, her concentration broken by this change. Her eyes narrowed. I could almost see the gears turning inside her head. Then she spoke, her eyes never going back to normal.

"The necklaces are acting like magnets. They must be!" She tested this theory by sliding over to me until my butt was touching hers. It was intimidating, really. Even though Lae was a bit smaller than me, I still felt as if she were some bully trying to squash me in the corner. Especially since she was staring at me with this intense face that reminded me of Mrs. Roy about to blame me for something I clearly hadn't done. But she was right about the necklaces being magnets. My jewel slammed into hers as soon as the two were close enough together. For the first time, I got a good look at Lae's jewel. It was not blue like mine, but spring green, and shaped like a leaf. I wondered what the others' jewels looked like.

"That's it!" Lae actually smiled. "Everybody, meet me in the center!" She got on her hands and knees and started crawling, however, she was stopped almost immediately as I was still sitting in the corner and was now connected to her. "Come on!" she urged. I sighed and crawled over to her. Rennoc was the first one in the center. Lae and I met him there, and our necklaces connected to his. Then Nika crawled over and was attached to the three of us. We had formed a circle, but there was one empty spot. The new boy then crawled over and filled it in. His necklace shot up and connected to ours.

At once, there was a huge blinding flash of light, except it didn't blind me like it should have, and traveled much slower than normal light. It started in the center where our necklace jewels were attached. Like a large balloon, the light grew bigger and bigger, until we were all inside of it. Bright, white light was all I could see. Everything was light, and yet my eyes didn't seem bothered by it one bit. It was the strangest thing. Then the light went out. It was gone, just like that. I almost doubted I'd seen it at all, and I would have, had I not had enough time to read everyone's faces before the next strange thing happened. They all wore pretty much the same expression, confused, scared, maybe slightly angry, and a tiny bit excited. That was exactly how I felt, and it made me feel better to know that I wasn't the only one who had experienced the abnormal light.

Another ball rose from the five necklaces, but this one was not light. It was made of colors, swirling around the ball like smoke – red, blue, brown, green, and white. Then it split into five bubbles, one of each color – red, blue, brown, green, and white. The blue floated towards me. It was the same aqua blue color as the jewel on my necklace. The same color as my mother's eyes. A lump grew in my throat, but it was quickly chased away and replaced with excitement and fear and anticipation of what was to come. The blue bubble halted directly in front of my face. Part of me wanted to reach out and grab it, but somehow I knew I shouldn't. The bubble began to rise. I followed it with my eyes until it froze again mere inches from the top of my head.

Looking around, I saw the other bubbles above my friends' heads – green above Lae, red above the new boy, white above Rennoc, brown above Nika.

The bubbles dropped. No sound, no warning, it just happened, and I was totally unprepared. I felt a rush of coldness and warmth at the same time flood over my body. Starting at the tip of my head, going down to my toes.

Then I was gone.

I was flying somewhere above the ocean. I could feel the sun on my back. See it reflected in the perfect blue sea. I could hear huge waves in the distance, but instead of making me nervous, it soothed me. I knew nothing could harm me while I was at sea. I felt the cool sea breeze on my back and smelt the salt in the air. It was paradise. I wanted to stay with the sea forever, but then, just as quickly as it had come, the vision was over.

I was still sitting on my knees in the center of the box with my friends. Our necklaces had disconnected. They were no longer vibrating, no longer glowing. It was as if nothing strange had ever happened, but I knew it had. So did the others.

"What ... just ... happened?" Rennoc asked. We all looked at Lae for answers, but she just frowned and shook her head.

"I don't think this is what happened to the untalented last year," said Nika hesitantly.

"Or the year before that." I added.

"Maybe we're special," suggested the new boy.

Suddenly, I had a thought. I counted the people in the circle. There were five of us. I sighed in relief, but then my stomach lurched. There'd been five of us *before* the new boy showed up. Panicking slightly, I tried to figure out who was missing.

"Where's Alyk?" I asked urgently. The others seemed surprised by my remark. They hadn't noticed that he was gone. I quickly scanned the box for the boy, and I saw him sitting in the same spot as he'd always been by the wall opposite the door. Relief washed over me, before I realized that something was wrong. Though I could plainly see the confusion in his face, I could just as easily see the sadness and disappointment. Alyk lowered his gaze with big teary eyes. I followed his gaze with my own, and then I understood. Alyk didn't have a necklace.

It took a very long time to reach wherever we were going. There was nothing to do but talk, and wait, so that's what we did.

The new boy introduced himself as Haras. He had auburn hair and friendly brown eyes. He had dimples and he smiled a lot, which reminded me of Mira. I liked him. I liked all my new friends – I felt it was safe to call them my friends by this point. We'd decided that wherever we were going, whatever happened, we would stick together. Alyk included.

The entire time we talked, Alyk sulked in his corner. He didn't acknowledge me when I spoke to him. I asked him what was wrong, even though I had a pretty good idea. I couldn't see how *not* having a weird glowing necklace was so bad though. It's not like the rest of us were going to abandon him because of it. I tried to tell him this but all he did was look at me. At least it was something.

Eventually we all got tired of talking and just sat around in silence. I tried not to think about my mother, but it was really hard. I couldn't get her loving blue eyes out of my thoughts. I tried to hold my tears back, but they came trickling down my cheeks against my will.

Nika, who was now sitting beside me, looked over at me sadly. Then she did something none of my childhood friends had ever done – not even Mira. She put her long arms around me and squeezed me in a hug. Surprised, I put my arms around the girl and hugged back. She was shaking slightly, and I guessed she was crying too. I only let go when all the tears were gone from both our cheeks.

"We'll ... we'll be fine," said Haras uncertainly from across the box.

"Will we?" asked Rennoc, almost sarcastically. Haras didn't seem to be able to find a positive answer to that.

What seemed like about five hours later (although, according to Lae, it was only two) the train slowed, and came to a stop.

We were there. It couldn't be another stop in Mencia, because the villages in Mencia were only about fifteen minutes apart. Butterflies fluttered around inside my stomach. I was about to start my new life.

We waited in silence and anticipation. Even Alyk was suddenly alert. Finally, I heard voices.

"Think I should even check? There haven't been any for the past four months." The speaker was male, and he had a funny accent that I'd never heard before. Another man replied, but he was too far away for me to understand. "Alright, alright," the first man said, and the door opened.

It didn't take as long for my eyes to adjust this time. The man standing there was very large and intimidating. He whistled when he saw us all sitting around the sides of the box. "Whoa, there's a lot of you this time." I was scared to move. This guy sent chills down my spine. I immediately didn't trust him. "What're you waiting for? Out! Let's get this over with." My insides told me not to, but then, what did I have to lose? I stood up and walked outside to stand by the man. The others followed me.

We were in another train station. This one was much bigger than the one back home ... I stopped mid-thought. It wasn't my home anymore. I would start my life over in this new place. Once we were all outside, the man spoke again. "Good. Now come with me and don't say anything unless I tell you to."

He turned around and started walking towards a door on one side of the long hall. I glanced at Nika. She shrugged and started after him. The rest of us followed her.

I remembered what the man had said before opening the door of the box to let us out. *There haven't been any for the past four months.* Surely he hadn't been talking about the untalented. The Talent Gaining was only once a year.

We stopped for the man to talk once we got out the door.

"Welcome to Jesburgon," he said. I could hear the sarcasm in his voice. "I will be giving you the short but interesting tour, blah, blah,

blah, then it's on to the 'new arrival' barracks until you get your jobs assigned and then I can go home." Beside me, Haras opened his mouth to say something, but before he could get anything out, the man bared his teeth and growled at him like a wild dog about to attack. Haras winced, and closed his mouth. Nika was right behind me. I heard her sigh. The man shot her an evil glare.

"Right, let's get this over with," he said, and then he started down the dirt road.

For the whole 'tour' we followed the man around Jesburgon. It was a huge village. Probably even bigger than Mencia's main one, but other than that, it was pretty much the same as my old village. Once in a while, the man would mutter a word or two about something we passed. Something like "pond," or "food market," but other than that, I just tried to figure out Jesburgon by myself.

At one point, when I was looking behind me at an odd-looking building, I thought I spotted someone dressed in grey following close behind us. I looked again and the person was gone. I was a bit nervous about it, but I decided it had probably just been a trick of my imagination.

We were just getting to a third pond – there were quite a few in Jesburgon – when a boy not much older than me, came running up to our 'guide'.

"Winel! The boss sent me to get you," said the boy.

Winel groaned. "Not now, Locky. Can't you see I'm *very* busy today?" He put on a very fake grin, showing his ugly cracked teeth.

"Um, well, it's kind of urgent," Locky added.

"Urgent, eh?"

"And, well, you know how the boss is … " Locky glanced nervously at my friends and me as he said that.

Winel sighed. "Alright, alright! I'm coming."

Winel turned to us. "Don't do anything. I'll get someone else to take you to the 'new arrival' barracks. Until then … " He narrowed his eyes and scowled at us, then he and Locky jogged back up the path. We all started talking at once when he turned the corner.

"Boy, he was mean."

"This place is huge!"

"Is anybody else hungry?"

"I wonder what his boss wants."

"How long are we going to have to stand here?"

"Do you think anyone here has a talent?"

All of a sudden, there was a huge splash. I

jumped at the noise, and quickly scanned my surroundings for its source. Then I saw him. A little boy had fallen into the pond up ahead. He was moving his arms but he wasn't strong enough to swim back to his sister, who was frantically trying to grab him from the edge.

In seconds, I was there beside her. I didn't know how, but I had to help the boy. I reached out to him, but my arms were no longer than his sister's.

Time was running out. The boy was barely keeping his head above the water.

Without thinking, I plunged my hand into the pond. The water was warm, almost cozy. I grasped a handful of it and pulled it up towards me. The water should have leaked through my fingers, but it didn't. It was as though I was holding onto a solid object instead of liquid. Don't ask me how I knew what to do, all I knew was I had to help the boy, and I did just that. When I brought my hand above the water, the water around it came up as well. Like a big blanket, I pulled the water out of the pond and onto the grass beside it, where it streamed down to the dirt road to create a large muddy puddle. The boy got pulled over to us in the current. His sister grabbed him, and lifted him into her shaking arms.

As soon as she knew her little brother was safe, the girl stood up and took a few hesitant steps away from me. Fear plastered on her face.

She was scared of me.

The girl turned abruptly and ran away, with her brother still in her arms.

I was shocked by my own work. I turned around to see my friends standing behind me with wide eyes. They were almost as confused as I was, and *much* more surprised.

Rennoc was closest to me. He frowned. "I think you have some explaining to do, Lexa," he said.

CHAPTER 5

THE WHISP

"I don't know," I repeated for the third time. "It just happened."

Lae sighed. My friends had been asking me the same question over and over since I'd saved the little boy from the pond. "What happened?"

I was telling them the truth. I had no idea, but Lae didn't seem to like that very much. In her world, everything made sense. *I* didn't live in Lae's world and hardly *anything* ever made sense to me. "Well, there must be *something* you understand about the whole thing," she told me frantically.

"Yeah, I understood that that boy needed help," I said, getting annoyed.

"But nothing else?"

"Give up Lae, she doesn't know any more than you do," said Rennoc. Lae shot him an evil look, but she stopped talking.

Suddenly, I saw something moving to my left, right beside Alyk. My head snapped over to look but it was gone in an instant. Nika noticed my head turn.

"What is it?" She asked.

I hesitated. "I don't know."

Lae frowned and narrowed her eyes at me. She opened her mouth to say something.

"Lae," warned Rennoc.

Just then, Haras's eyes grew wide and his mouth dropped open. He lifted his hand and pointed behind me. The others all looked at the thing he was pointing at in curiosity. Their first impressions of it were exactly the same as Haras's. All except Alyk, who frowned as if he couldn't tell what was so different about whatever they were looking at.

Slowly, cautiously, I turned around. Standing in front of me was a girl about my age. She had very long black hair and a pretty face with perfect lips and long dark eyelashes, but the fact that she was so beautiful wasn't why my friends were gaping at her. The girl was colorless. She was all black-and-white. Her eyes and lips were light gray, so were the few freckles that went across her nose. Her skin was very, very pale. In fact, it was completely white, and that wasn't all. She seemed to blur with her surroundings, as if she weren't solid, like a ghost. I wanted to ask, "What are you?" but I knew that would have sounded rude, so instead I started to say, "Who are you," but Rennoc beat me to it.

"What are you?" he asked. Unfortunately, Rennoc did not have a very good sense of what is rude – either that or he simply didn't care. Fortunately, the girl didn't seem to take it personally. In fact, ever since I'd seen her, she hadn't made any facial expression whatsoever.

"I am a whisp," she replied. Her voice was dull. It was like there was something missing from it; kind of like a robot, but it was still smooth like a regular person's voice.

"Who are you talking to?"

We all turned to look at Alyk. He glanced at me strangely, as if he expected me to shout out, "Ha! Fooled you!" But then he quickly looked back at the whisp when he saw my expression and realized that we weren't kidding. Then it dawned on me. He wasn't looking *at* the whisp; he was staring straight through her. Alyk couldn't see her.

"He cannot see me," said the whisp. Well duh, we'd kind of already figured out that much. "I am surprised that even you can see me." She didn't seem surprised. Her facial expressions hadn't changed and neither had her nearly robotic voice.

"What do you mean?" Haras asked.

"You're saying that nobody else but us can see you?" Lae said.

"It appears so, yes," replied the whisp.

"But ... how is that possible?" asked Haras.

"We're not special," added Nika.

"Think again."

I didn't know what she meant. Nika was right. We were nothing special. Less than that, we were untalented. I turned to Lae for answers. Luckily, she seemed to have found one.

"Necklaces," she said confidently.

"What?" wondered Rennoc out loud.

"Think about it! You said yourself what happened on the train wasn't normal. We each have a necklace, and we can see Miss whisp here. Alyk doesn't have one, and he *can't* see her!" explained Lae proudly. Alyk lowered his head shamefully.

"Yes," said the whisp. "Perhaps you can help me."

Help? Help the whisp? But how? Nika was clearly thinking the same thing.

"How ... can we help?" she asked. The whisp hesitated.

"I must explain what is happening first."

"What's ... uh ... she saying?" interrupted Alyk. Apparently he couldn't see *or* hear the whisp.

"We'll tell you later," I said hurriedly. I didn't want to repeat the whisp's words every five seconds. Alyk sighed sadly.

"Alright, tell us!" said Rennoc impatiently. The whisp closed her eyes. She waited a few seconds, lost in her own memories, before beginning.

"I wasn't always a whisp. I used to be a girl – Lia was my name. I had friends, a family, a *life* ... " The whisp smiled peacefully, her eyes still closed. "But that all changed, the day of my thirteenth birthday. I was invited to the castle, as all children are on their thirteenth birthday, to meet Lord Dennek, ruler of Jesburgon. I went alone, because it's a rule. Now I wish I had broken it.

"Lord Dennek is cruel. I'd barely walked into the room when he pointed at me and I began to transform into this whisp form of myself. I left right away, horrified by the truth, but my family couldn't see me. Not the real me, anyway. They seemed to believe the old Lia was still with them, though I wasn't actually.

"I soon found out that there are more whisps. Their loved ones cannot see them either, only a version of them that isn't there at all, and every time a child has his or her thirteenth birthday, they go to the castle where Lord Dennek turns them into a whisp. It's been going on for almost a year, and as no one else can see us, we can't warn those whose thirteenth birthday approaches."

The whisp finished her story and we were all silent.

"That's awful," said Haras finally. His voice was almost a whisper.

"*What's* awful?" muttered Alyk.

"But how are we supposed to help?" asked Rennoc.

"More importantly, how are we supposed to know we can trust you? This could all be a trick!" exclaimed Lae.

"Do you really want to spend who knows how long at the 'new arrival' barracks?" I raised my eyebrows. "*I* for one know what I'd rather be doing."

I watched in amusement as Lae tried to remain 'cool' while she gave in.

"*Alright.* But don't say I didn't warn you."

She made a big show of rolling her eyes. We turned our attention back to the whisp.

"You came here today from one of the other places, correct?" asked the whisp.

"How do you know that?" I asked. I held my breath. I thought I knew what she would say.

"I have been following you ever since you got off that train." I knew it. The whisp must have been the person in gray I'd seen behind us. "The people where you come from have magical powers, at least that's what I've heard. If anyone can help us, it's them. Please, go back and alert your ruler. He's bound to do something."

We raced back to Jesburgon train station so fast; I almost forgot to tell Alyk why. "Have to ... tell King Trub ... truth ... Jesburgon ... awful place ... help us." I wasn't making much sense. The only thing on my mind was: get back to the train before it leaves. If it left without us, we'd have to *walk* all the way to Mencia. I wasn't exactly looking forward to that.

"Never mind," said Alyk angrily.

It took longer than it should have to reach that station because we kept getting lost without Winel, as terrible a guide as he was.

For the first time, I took a good look at the people. There were more than a few who were all grey and spoke to no one. They were all children. Around thirteen years old in fact. I wondered how Lord Dennek could do such a horrible thing to his people. It made me run faster.

Finally, we reached our destination ... just as the train pulled out of the station. Nika groaned, and Rennoc stamped his foot in disgust.

"Now what do we do?" I asked, hoping Lae would have a better solution than walking.

"We walk! Won't that be fun!" exclaimed Lae sarcastically.

"Oh, well. They wouldn't have let us back on the train anyway" said Nika.

"I'm sorry to put you through this," said a smooth robotic voice behind us. I didn't know how the whisp had gotten there so quickly. She hadn't run with us, and she didn't appear to be in the least bit out of breath.

"It's fine, no one should be treated like you have been," said Haras reassuringly. I think the whisp would have smiled, but I don't think she could. In other words, her face was just as expressionless as it had been when I first saw her.

"Well, it'll probably take us a day to walk all the way back to Mencia. We'd better get started," said Lae.

"Yeah. Bye ... uh ... whisp?" I said, not sure what to call her.

"Call me Lia," she replied, answering my unasked question.

Half an hour later, we were silently walking in the woods. I had no idea where we were. Everything looked the same to me. I thought we were walking in circles. That is why *I* did not lead our group – Lae did. She seemed to know exactly which way to go to get back to Mencia, and knew roughly how much time it would take. Still, I had concerns.

"Haven't we passed this tree already?" I asked.

"Nope," said Lae confidently, without even looking at the tree I was pointing at. "That tree has much darker leaves than previous one did."

I looked more closely at the leaves. They didn't seem darker to *me*. We continued in silence for a few more minutes, before Alyk spoke.

"So, we're going back to Mencia because the ruler of Jesburgon is turning all the kids into ghost people that no one but you guys can see?"

We all nodded.

"And we're doing this because … we don't want to be turned into one of these?"

I shook my head. "We need to tell King Trub. He'll do something. I know he will … "

"But, why did that invisible thing …" started Alyk.

"Whisp!" interrupted Lae. "She is a *whisp* and her name is Lia."

"Okay, *whisp*. Why did the *whisp* come to *you*? Why not anyone else?" I noticed a change in his voice when he said "you", kind of as if he hated saying that word.

"Because we're the only ones she *can* tell," said Nika. "No one but us can see her, remember?"

"Not even her family," added Haras sadly.

I couldn't imagine not being able to talk to my family ever again – especially my mother. Then I remembered that I would, in fact, never see or speak to her again, whisp or not. The lump in my throat started to grow again. *No,* I thought. I wouldn't cry this time. But it was too late to stop the tears from coming. They trickled down my cheeks against my will. This time it wasn't loud. Actually, apart from the tears trickling down my cheeks, it was hard to tell I was crying at all. I fell to the back of the group so that no one would notice, but I was too late. Haras's eyes filled with concern, as soon as they connected with mine.

"What's wrong, Lexa?" He spoke softly, as if I were a very fragile vase that he didn't want to break. The others stopped walking. All eyes were on me. I tried to swallow back my tears, but it didn't work very well.

"I'm sorry," I said, looking down at the forest floor. "It's just … my mother … she gave me my necklace before my Talent Gaining. Then I was taken away … and I never got to thank her." It was true. I'd said, "I love you", but not "Thank you". It made me feel so guilty. I had expected them to roll their eyes and keep walking, but that's the opposite of what they did.

Haras put a hand on my shoulder. "It'll be alright," he said.

"I miss my mom too," Rennoc admitted.

"It's okay to be sad," added Nika.

"You'll see her again, I promise," said Lae. It was unlike Lae to say something that was so obviously untrue, but somehow, it still made me feel better.

Dusk came faster than I had hoped, and we decided that it was time to make camp. We found a nice spot to sleep – at least as nice a spot as you can get in the middle of the woods. The soil was dry, and it didn't have too many rocks. The tree branches in the area were thicker, so we would be protected if it rained. Then we faced the next challenges – making a fire and, more importantly, finding some food. None of us had eaten since that morning, and we were pretty hungry.

"Here's the plan," said Lae. "We split up, look for sticks to use for a fire, and possibly berries growing naturally, but don't go too far, and don't eat anything without my seeing it first."

"Since when did you become the boss?" muttered Rennoc, but we did as we were told. I wondered how Lae could possibly know which berries were poisonous any more than the rest of us, but she *did* seem to know a lot about being in the wild, so I let the thought slip away.

I wandered around for a bit, finding quite a few sticks, but hardly any were suited to starting a fire. I found no berries, or any other food for that matter. Eventually, I made my way back to 'camp' with about four twigs in my arms. Everyone was already there, except for Nika. I dumped my sticks in the small pile that they'd made – apparently, they'd had no more luck than me. We stared at the pile forlornly. Haras sighed.

"How are we going to make a fire with this?" asked Alyk hopelessly.

Just then, a twig snapped behind us. I whipped around in surprise, my heart racing. I relaxed when Nika came into view. I started to turn back towards the pile of sticks, but then I looked back, wondering if I'd really seen what I thought I'd seen. I had. In Nika's arms were sticks. Not just three or four, but a whole stack. I opened my mouth to ask where she'd found all of them, but Rennoc beat me to it – for the second time that day.

"Where did you get all those sticks?"

Nika's cheeks went red. She walked over to the pile and added her sticks to it before answering honestly. "I didn't find them," she confessed. "He did." She pointed to where she'd come from. A tiny squirrel bounded out and over towards her. Nika crouched down and put her hand out. The squirrel dropped a stick into it and Nika put it in the pile. She petted the squirrel as if she did it every day. I pinched myself, but I couldn't wake up from my strange dream, because it wasn't a dream at all. That's when I noticed Nika's necklace. It was glowing, like on the train. But not in the same way that it had on the train. This was different — a warm light-brown glow that brought back sweet memories of chasing wild rabbits around behind my house.

"Nika," I said. "Your necklace. It's glowing."

"Just like yours was when you pulled that little boy out of the pond," noticed Alyk. I gave him a look that asked why he hadn't mentioned that before, and he shrugged guiltily.

"Weird," said Haras. For once Lae didn't have anything to add.

We all sat down in a circle around the stick pile. The squirrel scampered up Nika's arm and onto her shoulder. She didn't seem to mind; in fact, I think she *liked* having him there. I certainly wouldn't.

"Well, this fire isn't going to light itself," said Lae. She crawled forward and picked up two sticks. She rubbed them together, hoping to get a spark, but her efforts were in vain.

"Here, let me try," said Haras. He crawled forward and picked up two sticks like Lae. He'd only touched them together when, without warning, they erupted into flames. I shrieked in surprise. Lae dropped her sticks and scooted backwards, away from the fire. Even Haras pulled the sticks away from each other with a strange look on his face. They went out immediately.

"Do it again," said Rennoc, amazement in his voice. Very slowly and carefully, Haras brought his sticks back together. The flames formed once more. He threw his sticks on the pile, and the others caught fire as well.

"Wow," said Haras softly. His red necklace was glowing.

CHAPTER 6

THE MIRROR

"Something strange is definitely happening," said Haras.

Lae nodded without taking her eyes off the fire. "It always leads back to the necklaces," she said.

"Well not everything," said Rennoc. "What about lord Dennek?" He raised his eyebrows.

"Dennek's beside the point right now," said Lae. "We're talking about something entirely different."

"Oh, so there's nothing strange about an evil lord turning kids into ghost-like forms that no one, apart from us, can see?" Rennoc added, sarcastically. Alyk shifted uncomfortably at the word "us".

Lae finally took her eyes off the fire to glare at Rennoc. "You know what I meant," she said coldly.

Rennoc crossed his arms and focused on the tree to his left. "I have no idea," he said, though obviously just to annoy her. Lae narrowed her eyes. She opened her mouth to say something – probably bad – and I braced myself for the upcoming fight.

"Stop!" yelled Nika. I made a silent note to thank her later. "Do you realize how ridiculous this is? Arguing over something so small right now? We have to work together if we want to survive the next few days! We have to get back to Mencia to tell King Trub about Lord Dennek." Her squirrel friend seemed to agree with her. He scampered up on top of her head and made some angry squirrel noises. They sounded like squeaky barks. "Tweep thinks so too," said Nika, with no hint of humour in her voice.

"Tweep?"

"That's his name."

"Why did you name him Tweep?"

"I didn't name him. He told me his name."

We got to Mencia in the late afternoon the

next day. We heard the noise before we saw it; people yelling, animals mooing, oinking, clucking, neighing and bleating, something big crashing into something else ...

We'd ended up at the edge of Leapton, more commonly known as Mencia's main village, which was its biggest and most crowded – not to mention its loudest, if you haven't already noticed – but that was good. King Trub's castle was located in the center of the village.

There was a long line of huge bushes separating the forest from the farm next to it. Quietly, so as not to alert anyone who might be hanging around on the other side, we crept up to the bushes and attempted to peer through them. But they were so thick that we couldn't see a thing on the other side – much less get through *to* the other side.

"Now what do we do?" said Rennoc, verbalising what was on all of our minds. No one answered. We couldn't just keep walking along the hedge until we reached the end because it went on for so long that my eyes couldn't see where it ended. It would probably take another day to get inside Mencia.

Then Lae approached the bushes. She put her hand up, and hesitated. I wondered if she would try to climb over. She placed her hand on the plant delicately, and the twigs in that area curled back so that there was a small hole, a few inches wide. I gasped. We'd seen some pretty weird stuff so far, but this was new.

Lae brushed her hand over the bush in an arch shape. The branches inside the arch twisted and curled outwards, creating the figure Lae had drawn. In no more than thirty seconds, I was staring at a doorway made through the bush into Mencia. It looked like a scene straight out of a fairy tale. It was only after the branches had stopped moving that Lae turned around. It was then that her green necklace's glow faded.

"Wow," said Alyk softly.

"Thanks," said Haras. Lae smiled at him, and his face brightened considerably in return.

One by one, we stepped through the hole into Mencia. We came out on a small farm. To our left was a large, grassy field where a herd of cows was grazing. Immediately to our right was a big wooden barn, and there were a few more buildings in the distance.

The door to the barn opened and a man walked out. He was a young man – tall and slim, with curly blond hair and a pleasant smile. I held my breath and waited for him to notice us, but the man turned away and set off towards one of the houses behind the barn, without giving us a second glance. He whistled as he walked.

I exchanged confused looks with my friends. So apparently, kids wandering out of the woods onto his property happened all the time?

I jumped as someone tapped me on the shoulder. I turned around and Nika pointed across the cows' field to a wooden fence, and beyond that, a dirt road. That's where we're headed.

"Which way?" I asked when we were safely outside the farm. Lae shrugged. Without waiting for an answer, she turned left and started walking down the dirt road. The rest of us decided we should probably follow her.

We'd passed two more farms before the houses started getting closer together, indicating that we were approaching the castle. Soon there were houses everywhere, on both sides of the road. The houses got bigger as well, the closer we got to the center of the village. This was where the wealthy people of Mencia lived.

We passed a few groups of children running around and enjoying the sun – which had been hiding for the past couple days. The weird thing was, the children didn't seem to notice us. It was as if we weren't there at all. Once, I accidently walked straight through a 'fort' that two young girls were building – which was pretty much just a circle of stones in the middle of the road – and they didn't even look at me.

We reached the castle without any problems at all, for which I was grateful, but I had a nagging thought at the back of my mind. This was too easy. What if Lae was right? What if this was all just a cruel trick?

We stood in front of the huge doors of the stone castle, waiting. There were guards on either side of the doors, but just like everyone else in the village, they paid us no attention whatsoever.

"Uh, excuse me?" Haras said after we had waited there awkwardly for a good few minutes. "We'd like to see King Trub please."

The guards showed no sign that they'd even heard him.

Getting impatient, Rennoc strode over to the guard on the right and waved his hand in front of his face. The guard stared straight ahead. Rennoc came back to us and shrugged.

"Maybe they're not real?" he said. Just as he'd finished speaking, the doors to the castle swung open and a woman carrying an empty basket hurried out. A maid. The two guards – whom Rennoc had just suggested were unreal – each grabbed a door and pulled it fully open so that they wouldn't slam shut and crush the woman.

Then I had an idea, but I had to act fast if I was to succeed.

"Come on!" I said as loud as I dared. Then I ran to the doors, dodging the maid – who also acted as if I didn't exist – and pushed my back against one of the doors, keeping it open. I felt the full weight of the door on my back as the guard let go of it. The door was very heavy. I knew I would only be able hold it for few seconds. Luckily, Lae had figured out my plan. She sprinted past me into the castle. The rest of my friends followed her. Alyk was the last to pass me.

Suddenly, the door's weight increased immensely as the guard – probably annoyed because the door wouldn't close – gave it a shove, and I was thrown inside. I collapsed to my knees in relief. We'd gotten into the castle, which was one less thing to worry about.

"Good thinking Lexa," I looked up to see Alyk smiling shyly at me. I smiled back as he helped me to my feet.

"Somehow I don't think those guards are fake, Rennoc," said Nika as she stared around the cavernous room.

I had not expected the inside of the castle to look as it did. It wasn't very … grand. The ceiling wasn't low, but it wasn't as high as I'd thought it would be. There were no windows, and no decorations other than a line of portraits on the dark gray wall. Each portrait was of a different man, yet they were all similar in some way, so I assumed they must be related.

"No, they're definitely real," said Haras.

"But then why …" I started to say, but Lae interrupted me without waiting to hear the rest of my question.

"I don't know."

Rennoc smirked. "Lae doesn't know something?" he teased, pretending to be astonished. If looks could kill, Rennoc would have been dead before he'd even stopped laughing. The glare Lae shot him was absolutely terrifying.

The door opened again and the guard by my door poked his head through.

"There's no one here," he said.

"Forget it. It was probably just the wind," the second guard called from outside. The first guard frowned and closed the door again, mumbling something about there being no wind.

"If I were a king, where would I be?" Lae asked herself. I looked around at our options. There were several passageways leading out of the entrance hall, and none of them would appeal to me if *I* were a king.

"I know how to settle this!" declared Haras. He walked into the middle of the room and squeezed his eyes shut. Then he held out his arm and pointed straight ahead. Haras started spinning in circles.

"Seriously?" Lae rolled her eyes. I tried my best not to laugh. Haras stopped spinning and opened his eyes, stumbling a bit, dizzily. He wasn't pointing anywhere near a passageway.

"Right, this way!" said Rennoc. He started towards the hallway directly *behind* Haras. Naturally, the rest of us followed him.

The hallway Rennoc had chosen went on and on, with no other rooms or connecting passageways. Yet we kept walking. I wasn't sure how, but now I was certain that King Trub would be at the end.

Finally, we reached the end of the hallway, where we found a strange-looking door, carved out of some dark wood. Nika pushed it open and we all walked inside. It was a large space, almost as big as the entrance room. It was fairly dark, and there were no windows, just a few torches on the wall. Scattered around the room on tables and shelves, and even on the floor, were all kinds of strange objects: a mirror that seemed to change color, a bowl filled with large gold coins, a silky, silver top hat …

That wasn't all. In the corner was a tall man. He had dark hair with strips of gray and a neatly trimmed beard. He clasped his hands together and smiled coldly when we noticed him.

"King Trub," whispered Alyk behind me.

No.

This couldn't be the King Trub I'd heard so much about. I refused to believe it. My teachers had said he was handsome and kind, like a hero from a storybook. He had helped my village with so many things we wouldn't have been able to do by ourselves.

This man looked cruel. Like the *villain* in a storybook. His eyes were a dark brown – almost black. They pierced me like daggers.

I did not trust him. Not one bit.

"Well, sit down," the king said. His voice was icy. Like a frost sweeping over my body, freezing my insides. He gestured towards six chairs arranged around an expensive-looking black stone table.

It was almost as if …

"I've been waiting for you."

My heart skipped a beat. The edges of Trub's lips curled upward in a sly smile. My insides churned. I took a deep but silent breath and sat lightly on the edge of the closest chair. My friends took my lead and did the same. Alyk sat right beside me. He was taking shaky, uneasy breaths. Across from me, Nika's eyes darted around the room, as if she expected something to jump out from behind a bookshelf or a suit of armour. At first glance, I didn't think Tweep was still with her that she had left him outside. But as I looked closer I saw movement in her hair. I wondered briefly how Nika could stand a rodent perched on her neck. I wished *I* could hide in someone's hair.

Finally, Haras somehow found the courage to break the silence. "If … if you've been waiting for us, then you must know *why* we've come."

King Trub sighed. He walked across the room. Slowly, he picked up the colour-changing mirror and brought it back to us. "The Seer is an amazing talent, don't you think?" He stared down at the mirror as he said those words, then he looked directly at me. My toes scrunched together in my shoes. I realized that he wanted me to respond.

"I ... yes ... I suppose," I said. The king took a few steps towards me. He looked down upon me intimidatingly and my insides twisted into knots. I felt as small and helpless as Tweep. I must have looked like it as well, because a cold smile crept its way onto Trub's face.

"Why don't you see for yourself?" he said mysteriously in his frosty voice. He laid the mirror on the table in front of me. The king didn't tell me what to do. He didn't have to.

I held my breath. Very slowly, my heart beating three times faster than normal, I leaned over and peered into the mirror. All I saw was my reflection – the same wavy chocolate brown hair and heart-shaped face as always – until I was right over the top of it, looking into my own round blue eyes.

It shocked me.

They appeared before my eyes so quickly and suddenly, like a flash of light. And terrible things they were. My friends walking away from me. Leaving me alone. A man, who looked almost like a younger version of King Trub, holding my necklace in front of his face and laughing like a madman. My mother, with intense fear in her eyes – something I'd never seen before. A silver dagger flying through the air, straight towards her heart.

I pulled away from the mirror in shock, not wanting to see any more. I nearly fell off the chair I was sitting on, but Alyk caught me by my arm. I stared at the floor and did not look up. I couldn't face my friends just yet.

Trub chuckled at my behaviour. "Strange, isn't it," he said.

I didn't answer. My sweaty hands were trembling uncontrollably and it took all my effort not to burst into tears.

I wondered if that was actually what happened to Seers, or maybe King Trub had just shown me those horrible things to scare me.

"Now, about why you are here …" said Trub. "The mirror *shows* me important things, but it does not *tell* me anything."

"So, you don't know why we're here?" asked Lae. There was a short pause. I didn't see it, but I assumed that Trub nodded because Lae spoke again. "Well, you see … we've come from Jesburgon … "

"You're untalented," Trub interrupted her. His voice was now full of hatred. I forced myself to look up. The king's face had also darkened.

"Uh …" Lae was lost for words.

"Yes, but *you* aren't," said Haras thinking quickly. "We were hoping you would help us."

Trub scowled. "And why, *untalented* child, would I help you?"

"Please sir, the ruler of Jesburgon is turning children into ghost-like forms of themselves!" Nika spoke up.

"Nobody can see them but us," added Rennoc.

The king's ears pricked up. He turned his head around slowly towards Rennoc with his jet-black eyebrows raised. He studied Rennoc closely, as if there was something about him that he'd missed before.

"I'm sorry," he said, exaggerating enthusiasm. "I must have misheard you. Did you say nobody but you can see them?"

Rennoc had blown it. We were speechless.

Out of the corner of my eye, I saw Nika's hand fly up instinctively to cover the light brown jewel of her necklace. Unfortunately, the motion was enough to catch Trub's attention as well. He looked at Nika suspiciously. She removed her hand when she realized what she had done, but the damage was already done.

The king's eyes lit up when he saw Nika's beautiful jewel. He took a few slow-moving steps around our table to the tall girl. He bent over to examine her precious necklace.

"Where did you get that?"

"It's a family heirloom," replied Nika stiffly, her body rigid and her eyes unmoving.

"Ah, I see."

Without coming out of his hunched-over position, Trub's eyes skimmed around. They landed on each of us in turn and located our necklaces. A smile grew on Trub's face, but this one was different from his previous one. This smile was real. Real, and wicked.

Everything happened so fast that I barely had time to process it all. Trub's hand darted out and grabbed Nika's necklace. She screamed in alarm. Tweep sprang out of her hair at his friend's cry. He landed on Trub's face with his tiny sharp claws outstretched. The man howled in pain. He removed his hand from Nika's necklace to use both hands to pry the animal off. But Tweep held on, digging his claws into the king's flesh. He began to claw at king Trub's eyes. Trub staggered backwards, howling loudly. He bumped into a shelf behind him. The objects on the shelf wobbled precariously, and a beautifully painted china bowl fell to the floor where it smashed into little pieces. Its contents – half a dozen large gold coins – skidded across the floor. Then Haras was there.

Haras laid his palm on the side of the shelf, and just like the twigs in the woods, it burst into flame. I felt the heat immediately. Trub's screaming intensified as his clothes caught fire.

Someone grabbed my arm. I whipped my head around and saw a pair of intense dark brown eyes staring back at me.

King Trub.

Adrenaline rushed through my body. I pulled away. He didn't try to stop me.

But wait …

King Trub was *behind* me. Then who … ?

I relaxed a bit. It was just Alyk.

"Come on!" he urged. The others were already running out the door. Alyk and I followed them without a second thought, leaving king Trub burning and clutching his bleeding face where Tweep had scratched it.

We sprinted down the hallway and into the entrance hall. No one spoke. My only thought was to get out. Somehow I knew that I could not let King Trub take possession of my necklace.

We burst through the heavy double doors of the castle and were met by a cry of alarm from the startled guards. I just about heard the one on the left say to his buddy, "Call *that* the wind?"

To my dismay, I soon discovered I was one of the slowest members of our group. Nika was naturally fast with her extra long legs, but Rennoc was a close second. To my surprise though, Lae was right behind them. That girl seemed to be good at everything. Haras and I, on the other hand, were lagging behind, with Alyk a short way ahead.

This wasn't like running back to the train station in Jesburgon. This time, I knew some terrible fate awaited me if Trub caught up. For one thing, he would get my necklace, which simply could not happen. For another, and far worse, it could mean death for all of us.

We ran past the houses, and the children playing in the road. Just as before, no one noticed us. It was as if we didn't exist.

After what felt like an eternity of trying to keep up with my friends, the last of the small houses disappeared, giving way to the peaceful countryside. I could hear birds chirping happily. They made me relax a bit more, we were almost there, almost free. Just a few more minutes of running …

Then King Trub was in front of us.

Impossibly, he just appeared out of thin air. One moment our path was clear, the next it was blocked by the man I had hoped to never see again.

Nika let out a high-pitched screech and skidded to a halt just a few feet from the angered king. Teeth gritted, Trub shoved something into his pocket. He started towards us, hands in tightly squeezed fists. With his burned clothes, ash-splotched skin, and bloodied face and hands, Trub looked like zombie. We were doomed.

Out of the corner of my eye, I spotted a pond. An idea began building itself inside my brain. The pond was small, but it would work. Using all my concentration, I reached out to the pond. Just as I had when I'd first used this strange talent, I knew exactly what to do.

My hand was a magnet. The water flew out of the pond and towards me under some invisible force. At the last second before it reached me, I moved my arm, and the water changed its course in midair. My friends gasped as the liquid flew over their heads and collided with king Trub with such force that it knocked him right over.

"Go!" I shouted.

This time, instead of using my hand like a magnet, I used it in the opposite way. Almost effortlessly, I pushed some of the water away to clear a path large enough for us to sprint through single file. Lae didn't have to be told twice. She took off past King Trub – who was still struggling to breathe while surrounded by water – and I followed her, with the others close behind.

Just when we could see the farm up ahead, and almost taste freedom, I heard Nika scream again. I stole a glance behind me.

He was right there. Catching up with every passing moment. And there were no ponds sitting around this time.

Rennoc stopped running.

Trub was getting closer. Closer still.

I acted without thinking.

I ran towards Rennoc, who was just standing there, staring straight ahead at nothing in particular. I had no clue what he was doing, but I could not let my friend be taken by the mad king.

It was a race now. I did not know who would reach Rennoc first – Trub or me. Then Rennoc acted.

He swivelled around to face the king and held up his hands, as if telling him to stop. Surprisingly, Trub did just that. But not willingly. An invisible force was pushing him back. He closed his eyes, his dark hair being blown off his face.

Wind. I realized. Rennoc was pushing the air at Trub, preventing him from coming any farther.

Rennoc took a few steps back, hands still raised, but the huge gust of wind hardly weakened. His steps sped up, until he was running again, with his right arm still directed to the king behind him.

We ran across the farm and through Lae's arch in the bush. She swept her hand across the opening and the twigs grew back into place. It looked just as it had before.

CHAPTER 7

THE DEAL

I collapsed against the hedge as soon as I knew we were safe. I could hear King Trub yelling at us from the other side, but I didn't care. There was no way I would be going back there any time soon.

I just wanted to stand there and catch my breath. I felt so angry I wanted to cry, but I didn't. I *couldn't*. Not this time. I'd already shown my friends enough weakness by crying. I had to be strong.

I felt a frantic tapping on my shoulder. I looked up to see Lae gesturing dramatically for me to follow her. She wanted to talk, and we could not do that in an area where Trub could hear us. I felt the heat from the early afternoon sun suddenly vanish from my back as we disappeared into the shadows of the trees.

Stress. Confusion. Frustration. Nothing made sense. My thoughts gathered in my eyes in the form of tears that threatened to fall.

It's going to be fine, I told myself. *We'll figure it out.* Slowly, the tears backed away.

We followed Lae through the forest until I could no longer hear the sounds of the Mencian farm. Lae turned to face us, her expression serious. She meant business.

"We need to talk." She spoke like a mother addressing her young children.

Well, obviously. The king of Mencia was mad and greedy. He clearly hated the untalented and wouldn't be helping Jesburgon any time soon. Now we had to go back empty-handed. I could already see the disappointment in Lia's eyes – only her eyes because her face never showed any emotion. I could already feel the shame. I hated the feeling. But what troubled me the most were the things Trub's mirror had shown me.

I could still see it all. My friends abandoning me, the man holding my necklace, my mother with a dagger flying at her heart. I made a decision then that I would never tell the others what I'd seen. It would just distract them from more important things ... like it was doing to me.

Lae picked up the green jewel of her necklace and placed it in the palm of her hand for all of us to see.

"This is no ordinary jewellery. All of our necklaces seem to be giving us special talents – unlike any I've ever seen before.

I nodded, not wanting to speak for fear that I would burst into tears.

"I've had this since my parents gave it to me on my tenth birthday, but it didn't start glowing until recently," argued Nika.

Lae thought about it. Her eyes darted around as if she were visually connecting the dots. After a minute of silence, except for the leaves rustling in the light breeze, Lae replied.

"Remember back on the train? The necklaces kind of connected ... like magnets. That must have activated them or something."

I nodded again. I hadn't done any thinking, but she was right.

"Wait," said Nika. She set Tweep on the ground as she spoke. "The Globe of Tarahabi said we were all untalented. The Globe has never been wrong before."

"She's right," put in Rennoc.

I looked to Lae for an answer but Haras spoke instead.

"These aren't *our* talents," he realized. They belong to our necklaces. That's why the pendants glow whenever we use them."

A dreadful silence followed those words.

That must have been why King Trub wanted the necklaces so badly. They contained extraordinary talents. If one possessed them all, they would quite possibly have more power than the Seers. I promised myself that I would do everything I could to keep my beautiful blue necklace from falling into the wrong hands.

Realization hit me like a punch in the face and I gasped, attracting the attention of my companions.

"I ... yesterday, before my Talent Gaining ..." I started. "I met my village seer on my way to school. She told me ... she'd seen that I was in 'great danger'." I paused. "You don't suppose she was referring to my necklace, do you?"

There was more silence. I noticed Alyk half hidden behind Nika's rather lanky body. Though he was not contributing, I could tell he was deeply engaged in the conversation. His eyes darted from person to person, as if he were trying to predict who would speak next.

"What else did she say?" Lae pursed her lips.

"Uh ..." I struggled to remember Bya's exact words. "The enemy is better when ... uh ... the enemies are better ... no, *stronger* ... the enemies are stronger when they are together. Or something like that."

Rennoc looked up in horror. "What if King Trub and Lord Dennek are working together?"

Everyone was asleep – everyone but Alyk.

The boy sat with his back against a tree trunk and his legs hugged to his chest, watching his friends sleep.

His *friends*.

Was it really appropriate to call them that? *Companions* was probably a better word. Or even *fellow travelers*.

He didn't know how they could sleep after everything that had happened over the past two days. Alyk had been awake for quite some time last night as well.

He looked down at Rennoc who was asleep on his back beside Alyk. Rennoc's mouth was open and he was snoring loudly. His necklace poked out from his coat. Its beautiful stormy grey stone was lit up in the moonlight and it captured Alyk's gaze. The necklace looked like rain clouds swirling around inside a smooth, spherical glass.

He absent-mindedly wondered what it would be like to control the wind – to knock enemies to the ground with one simple wave of his hand. What would it be like to be so powerful? To be *unstoppable*? What would it be like … to have a talent? Alyk desperately wanted to know. He wondered what would happen if he put on the necklace. Would the talent transfer over to Alyk? Or would it remain with Rennoc? What would happen if he put on all *five* necklaces?

Alyk suddenly became aware of his hand inches away from the enchanting silver necklace. He pulled it away quickly, horrified by what he had been about to do.

Alyk scooted away from Rennoc. As far away from the others as he could get without leaving the makeshift camp. Even if they were not his friends, he still had to protect them from … *him*.

He closed his eyes and choked back a sob.

It had started a few years ago. Alyk had begun having new thoughts, which went completely against his normally optimistic personality. At first, he was able to keep the sly, snide comments to himself, but as time went by, 'New Alyk' – as he called it – seemed to grow stronger. It grew harder to push away the bad thoughts and replace them with the familiar good ones.

It was almost as if another person had invaded Alyk's body and mind, and was taking over, little by little.

He was afraid.

Sure, he was worried about King Trub and Lord Dennek, and the weird invisible things in Jesburgon. But he was terrified of what would happen when New Alyk overcame him eventually, and took charge of his actions, as well as his thoughts.

Not *if. When.* It would happen, sooner or later.

Alyk's fear was replaced by frustration. He should be able to defeat it. He just wasn't strong enough. *Why* was he not strong enough? He *should* be strong enough. He *had* to be strong enough, or else he feared everyone he knew and loved would be in danger. And it would be all his fault.

All his fault. The words echoed through his thoughts, letting the guilt settle.

He slammed his fist into the ground as hard as he could in an attempt to lessen the frustration. He nearly yelped in pain as he felt tiny sharp rocks dig into his skin, but the emotions did not fade.

Across the small camp, Nika twitched in her sleep, and Alyk held his breath, praying she wouldn't wake up and find him in a battle with his own emotions. Alyk waited a few moments, and when Nika remained still, he let out a defeated sigh.

He had to have some time alone – away from his companions; somewhere he couldn't accidentally wake them from their peaceful slumber.

Alyk stood up carefully. Without another thought, he turned and walked away from the sleeping friends. He didn't know where he was going. Only that he was walking away. Finally alone, he let all his emotions cave in on him. Tears filled his eyes and he let them fall. He continued to stumble through the woods so absent-mindedly, with his vision so blurred by tears, that it was a miracle he didn't bump into any trees or trip over any stray roots … until he did.

He fell to the ground and lay there, sobbing.

It wasn't fair.

If only he wasn't an untalented, life could be so much better. He could still be living merrily in his house back in Mencia with his forgiving parents and loving baby sister, Myanna.

Alyk could still remember that wonderful day last year when his sister was born.

He had always wanted a younger sibling. All the groups of siblings that he knew looked alike. Whenever someone new saw them together they would say "Whoa! You're siblings, right?".

Alyk looked nothing like his parents. They both had strawberry-blond hair and toothy smiles that did not explain Alyk's dark brown hair and near-black eyes. He had hoped that having a brother or sister with similar features to his would make him look like he was actually related to his family.

Unfortunately, as it turned out, Myanna looked nothing like him, but Alyk still held her close to his heart. On the worst of days, seeing his sweet little sister's adorable face always made him smile.

But all of that had been ruined the day of his Talent Gaining. If only it hadn't.

After what felt like ages, the tears stopped flowing, but the sadness remained, making him feel like he was sinking into the ground. Like he was drowning. His life was pointless. He should just lay here to die, and get it over with.

But what if there was still a part to come where everything got better? What if he had a chance to see Myanna again?

Alyk stood up. He should probably head back. Maybe try to get a few hours' sleep before the sun came up. He was extremely tired after all. He took a good look around at his surroundings, wondering which way was the way he had come.

There was a shallow stream on his right. He wasn't the least bit wet, so he must have come from the opposite direction.

Slightly pleased with himself, Alyk turned away from the stream to start making his way back. He had only taken a few steps when he realized how very thirsty he was. He quickly turned around and raced back to the refreshing water.

He kneeled down and cupped his hands to scoop the water into his mouth. As he drank, Alyk look up at the moon overhead. It was beautiful and soothing. He sighed and looked back down at the stream. He yelped and jumped to his feet, backing away.

There was a face staring up at him.

It was the face of a man who looked strangely like King Trub, except this man was younger – probably in his early twenties. He had a similarly shaped face and dark hair minus the strips of gray. His eyes were also the same as King Trub's. Like the dark, sinister ice of a frozen lake.

The face rippled with the water flow. It was a reflection in the stream. Alyk's heart skipped a beat as he glanced behind him, but there was no one there. He narrowed his eyes. Some people had the rare talent of being able to communicate through water. That must be what the man was doing. But why would he wish to speak with Alyk?

"Hello my boy." The man spoke with a soft, low vice, but that didn't mean it was friendly. "My brother told me you'd be heading this way."

His brother ...

"You're Lord Dennek," guessed Alyk, remembering Rennoc's suggestion that Trub and Dennek might be working together.

"Very good." Lord Dennek smiled, showing his teeth. They were white and unnatural.

"What do you want?" asked Alyk. He hoped that he looked braver than he felt.

The lord raised his eyebrows in a sly way. His long pause increased the tension level in the already uncomfortable conversation. "What do *I* want? It's not about what I want. It's what *you* want."

Suddenly, Alyk was overwhelmed by greed. All his thoughts of Myanna and his old life disappeared, leaving only the desperate need to get his hands on … those necklaces.

He knew what was happening. His worst nightmare was coming true. New Alyk was spilling those thoughts into his head, but this time it was different. This time it was *much* stronger. This time he couldn't stop it.

Lord Dennek watched the boy struggle. The corner of his mouth twitched upwards in a half-hidden, satisfied grin.

"I can promise you complete control over one of your … ah … *friends'* necklaces," persuaded Dennek.

In one big burst of energy, what was left of Old Alyk was shoved away. Something new and strange took complete control of the boy's mind … and body.

New Alyk took a step closer to the stream. From here he could see his own reflection as well as Dennek's. New Alyk's eyes were different. They were deeper, more solid, like tricky black ice.

"Keep going," he told Lord Dennek.

"I can give you talent beyond your wildest imaginings," said Dennek. "For a price, of course."

New Alyk did not hesitate. "What's the

deal?"

Lord Dennek grinned in a way that only villains can. "Your task is simple. Get the necklaces to me."

CHAPTER 8

THREAT

I awoke to my stomach growling painfully. I groaned softly and wondered what was for breakfast. And why had Oranah taken my blanket and pillow? I rolled stiffly onto my back and opened my eyes to see clear sky above me.

Everything came back at once and hit me like a punch in the chest. I was untalented. King Trub had some kind of seer's mirror. My necklace was magic. The children of Jesburgon were being turned into whisps. I would never see my mother again.

I bit my lip. It took all of my willpower not

to cry. I pushed myself up into a sitting position and took a deep breath to calm myself. Looking around the small clearing where we had slept, I noticed that I was one of the last to wake up.

Lae was saying something to the others, which couldn't have been very interesting because Haras was the only one listening. Well, I assumed he was listening by the way he was staring at her contentedly.

Nika looked mildly bored as she watched Tweep run back and forth across the clearing, and Rennoc was greedily feasting on a handful of juicy-looking red berries that he must have got from the bush beside him – which I definitely did not remember from the night before.

Alyk was now the only one still asleep. The quiet boy was curled up in a ball on the other side of the clearing, a good distance from the rest of us.

"Hey, Lexa's awake," Rennoc said, his voice muffled by the berries he had just stuffed into his mouth. He licked the juice off his fingers and my stomach growled ferociously, reminding me again of how hungry I was.

"Tell me that wasn't there last night." I pointed at the berry bush.

"It wasn't." Nika answered.

"Then how … ?"

"It was Lae," Haras said excitedly. "She was amazing!" Lae blushed, but did not say anything.

"It was pretty cool," admitted Nika. "She put her hand on the ground, and when she took it off, that bush started growing."

I crawled over to the bush and inspected its berries suspiciously. I could not remember ever seeing berries quite like these round, red ones before. I wondered if they were safe to eat and hesitated, but my stomach growled impatiently. I plucked a few and held them in my cupped hand.

"Try them, they're not bad," Rennoc urged. I picked up a large one between my thumb and forefinger, and hesitated once more.

"Oh, come on Lexa, they're not poisonous!" I quickly popped it into my mouth at Lae's surprising outburst. Juice squirted out of the berry as I bit down; sweet and sour at the same time. I was not a big fan of sour foods, but – probably because I was so hungry – it was the best thing I'd ever tasted. I stuffed the rest of my handful into my mouth and reached for more. Lae made a big show of rolling her eyes.

A soft groan drew my attention to where

Alyk lay, curled in a ball. I ate another handful of berries as I watched him sit up and rub his eyes sleepily.

"Morning," I said as I picked another bunch. "Have some breakfast."

The walk *to* Jesburgon definitely seemed more difficult than the walk *from* Jesburgon. My dress kept getting snagged on stray tree branches and I kept tripping over roots. There were so many more things to worry about as well.

Lae had resumed her very boring conversation. "You see, the leaves on this tree are more of a rich green than the leaves on that tree. That tree's leaves have a slight bluish tint to them, kind of like that patch of moss over there, which indicates ... " I tried to listen, mainly to keep my mind from wandering to other matters, but after a few minutes of her blabbering on about plant life, her voice had become nothing more than background noise to me.

"Tell me about ... tell me about your mother." I had been staring at my feet when Alyk came up beside me and asked the question, which, I must admit, took me aback. I looked up at him curiously. There was something about his dark brown eyes that just didn't seem right.

"It's just … the way you talk about her. She seems like a really nice person."

So I told him. I told Alyk all about my mother and our life together. Talking about it actually made me feel a bit better. Even though a great deal of unfortunate incidents had recently occurred in my life, I was reminded that good things had happened to me in the past, and so good things could happen again.

"Which village did you live in?" Alyk asked at some point. My village was called *Kaprota*, I told him, and although it was rarely referred to by its true name, all my schoolteachers had made sure it was drilled into my brain.

To this he smiled and replied, "I lived in Temner. Kaprota was the closest village to us."

I decided that the shy boy was friendlier than he seemed.

We stopped only once, partly because walking was tiring, and partly because, now that he knew Lae could grow food, Rennoc wouldn't stop complaining about his hunger pains. I didn't say anything, but I silently agreed with him.

So, after half an hour of putting up with his complaints, Lae scowled at Rennoc and said,

"Alright, we'll stop for a snack. And you'd better stop whining."

Lae knelt down in the dirt beside a small tree. She bit her lip, and placed her hand flat on top of the dry soil. After a few long seconds filled with suspense, she slowly raised it. A stem began to grow where Lae's palm had just been.

As Lae took her hand away, the little plant continued to grow taller, and branches grew from its side, twisting and curving as they expanded the plant. Next, buds began to form on each branch, which bloomed into little pink flowers, then turned into healthy green leaves. Then came the berries. My mouth began to water.

Blackberries were my favourite fruit, no contest, and these were the biggest, juiciest blackberries I'd ever seen. I was the first to sit and start rapidly picking.

Only Lae remained standing. She cleared her throat loudly to get our attention. She raised her eyebrows expectantly when she was certain all eyes were on her. I attempted not to giggle as the rest of us chorused, "Thank you Lae," as if we were six-year-olds at school again. Satisfied, Lae smiled smugly, briefly nodded once, then plopped down between Nika and Haras, crossed her legs, and began to eat. It was only after stuffing my mouth for the seventh time that I realized Alyk was missing.

Suddenly panicking, I took several deep breaths and carefully looked around to make sure he wasn't there. I swallowed my berries nervously.

"Guys, where's Alyk?"

"Here." I jumped when Alyk sat down beside me.

"Where were you?" I demanded. Alyk pointed to the woods behind us.

"Why?"

"Uh …" The colour drained from his face.

Rennoc snorted. "Really Lexa?" Then, in a slightly softer voice, he added, "He had to use the bathroom, silly."

"Yes," agreed Alyk, much too quickly in my opinion. I examined him closely. Though his 'offness' had faded a bit, there was still something not quite right about him. There was something in his eyes …

"Come off it Lexa, you're turning into Lae!" Rennoc said.

Lae slapped him.

We reached the edge of Jesburgon a few hours later, at dusk. I did not know that such a horrible place could appear so breathtakingly beautiful. The west sky was lit up with oranges and pinks of all shades as the bright sun descended behind the tall trees on the outskirts of the peaceful village. It was difficult to believe that dreadful things were happening here.

We walked slowly through the quiet streets of Jesburgon. Every now and then, we came across one person or another: a merchant packing up after a day of business, a couple on a romantic evening walk, a lonely whisp staring longingly into the window of a cute cottage-like house.

"Now what?" Haras said, breaking the silence.

I shrugged.

"We go find Lia … I guess," said Nika. "And tell her we failed to help," she added miserably.

I heard a small splash from the pond we were walking by – the same pond as the day before, I realized – and I turned my head to find out what had caused the disturbance.

A part of the water near the edge of the pond was swirling around in a small circle. I hurried over, closely followed by my friends, and we all watched in silence as the water rippled and bubbled, but made no noise. It was so quiet that if you hadn't been watching it, you wouldn't have notice it happening. I leaned in closer to see better. Despite the water's motion, I could still see my reflection clearly, though only for a second, because it began to change. Like a puzzle rearranging itself, part of me disappeared, and then was replaced with new parts. Soon, I was no longer staring at my own reflection, but at the reflection of a man. With his coffee black hair and freezing dark brown eyes, he looked like a younger replica of King Trub.

"K–King Trub?" I stammered. The man smiled, making me shiver.

"Not quite. I do resemble him greatly though, don't you think?" He spoke slowly, as if to make sure each word petrified us even more than the one before.

"Then … who are you?" Nika spoke up.

"I am Lord Dennek."

I sucked in my breath.

"What do you want from us?" Lae demanded bravely.

"Oh!" Lord Dennek pretended to look surprised. "Isn't it obvious?"

I narrowed my eyes.

"I want those precious talent-containing necklaces of yours."

Nika's hand went instinctively to her neck.

I clenched my hands into fists. "You'll

never get them," I growled to Dennek.

My necklace was more than just simple jewellery; apart from being talent embedded, it was a family heirloom, and a gift from my mother.

"Well, that's too bad," Dennek said in a mocking tone. "I guess you'll just have to suffer the consequences then."

I gulped. Consequences?

Lord Dennek seemed to read my expression. "Oh yes, consequences." I went numb with anticipation. "I'll give you … hmm … let's say until dawn to hand them over, or …" He paused dramatically. "She dies!"

With a soundless snap, the reflection changed again, and I saw a woman on the floor of a stone birdcage large enough for a person to stand up in. She looked up helplessly and I glimpsed her eyes. Her deep ocean-blue eyes that were the same color as my necklace.

It was my mother.

CHAPTER 9

HOPE IS LOST

I could barely make out Lae's blurry form a few feet away through my tear-filled eyes.

"We're not going."

Another burst of misery and hopelessness pumped through my body, affecting my chest – namely my heart – the most. This was deeper and more painful than the previous bursts of sadness. If we did not do as Dennek asked, my mother would be gone. Permanently. And Lae had just declared that we would not.

I instinctively wrapped my arms around my chest, as if I were shielding myself from anything that might hurt me more – physically and emotionally.

Nika put her arm around me. "It's not that we don't care," She spoke softly into my ear "It's just … " Her voice trailed off. I thought she might break into tears as well.

I heard Rennoc's voice somewhere to my left. "Well, I've never even *met* your mother." Then, perhaps realizing that his statement had sounded harsh, he quickly added, "I'm sure she's a wonderful person, but …" He trailed off.

But I knew what he'd been about to say. I could tell that he did not wish to sacrifice his necklace to save another human being – even if it was my mother. My sadness was tinged with anger.

I read each of my friends' faces, desperately trying to believe that *someone* agreed with me. In Nika's expression, I could see stress and a touch of sympathy. Rennoc, too, appeared sympathetic, but I could also detect a hint of shame in his eyes. Haras's face was full of sadness and sympathy as he stared directly at me, but when he realized I was looking at him, this was replaced with confusion and anxiety. His eyes darted around, and landed on Lae, as another emotion was added to the mix – one that I couldn't quite place.

Alyk's expression confused me. The strange aloofness I'd noticed before had returned, and it seemed to be messing with his emotions. It looked like he *wanted* to feel sympathetic, but something kept pushing the sentiment away – either another emotion or … something else. Also in his expression I could see fear, desperation and … need? I really had no idea what was happening inside my friend's head.

I looked over at Lae finally. If she felt any sympathy, she was hiding it well. She was indeed quite skilled at hiding her emotions, as I was just noticing now. The only thing I could make out was maybe slight annoyance, or impatience.

"Please, I don't want to lose …"

"It's a trap Lexa! Why can't you see that?" I tensed at Lae's sudden outburst. "Who knows if Dennek will even keep his part of the bargain? Think for a moment; this man has been turning children into ghosts for no apparent reason. Do you really think he wants our necklaces to do good?"

The small spark of anger inside of me burned brighter, the flame building with each word. Of course I didn't think Dennek would use our necklaces to do good, but how else could I get my mother back?

"Think of all the terrible things he could do with the power of all the elements in his hands. Just one of these talents alone is probably more powerful than any other. What damage could they cause when used together?"

I could now barely contain the angry flame in my chest.

"The thing is Lexa, some things just aren't worth the risk."

Something snapped. The anger surged through my body like electricity. It wanted out, one way or another.

My cheeks got hot, my hands clenched into fists. My whole body tensed as if I were readying myself for a fistfight.

Then I started screaming uncontrollably, words leaving my mouth before I'd even processed them in my mind, but I honestly didn't care. My mind was too fogged by horrible angry thoughts to be able to think straight.

"I'm tired of this! You're all selfish and cruel!" My voice was unfamiliar and shrill. "You don't care about me. You don't care that my mum is going to *die*! You only care about yourselves and your oh-so-special necklaces. And I hate you, *all* of you. Especially *you*!" I pointed sharply at Lae, and she staggered backwards a few steps, as if my finger were a spear, a bewildered expression on her face. "I liked you. I trusted you. I thought of you as my friends! I thought we were some sort of team! But I guess I was wrong about you. You're just going to let my mum *die*? You ... you don't deserve your necklaces!"

By this point the rest of the group had taken a few steps back after Lae. The five of them were now standing in a crooked line a few feet away, all looking very hurt. I could have – *should* have – stopped there, and if I were in my right mind I would have. But once the overwhelming anger had begun flowing freely out of me, it was pretty near impossible to stop until most of it had left my body.

"And you know what? I'm going to Lord Dennek to get my mum back anyway! It's probably best that you don't come, because you obviously aren't my *friends*!"

Silence.

A badly muffled sob made my eyes snap instinctively towards the sound. My words appeared to have cut Nika the deepest. The tall girl had her hand cupped around her nose and mouth. The tears I'd seen in her amber eyes now flowed freely down her cheeks. Seeing her like this almost made me want to take back everything I'd just said. *I* was the emotional one, not Nika.

Though she was still attempting to hide her emotions, I could tell that Lae felt deeply wounded as well. Her bottom lip trembled, and a vertical crease was visible between her eyebrows. Her eyes, once a brilliant shade of electric blue, were now greyish and dull, glassy with tears that she refused to let fall.

"Fine," Lae spat in an unfamiliar, unstable, high-pitched voice. "Go hand over your necklace to an evil man who probably won't even keep his promise of giving up your mother when you do so!" Her words were like a large heavy ball being thrown at me. They hit hard, and it hurt. "And don't expect us to go with you." She turned around sharply, and walked away swiftly, her wheat-blonde hair flying messily behind her.

Nika was the first to follow. Lae had only gone a few feet when she turned and went after her, looking at the ground in front of her to avoid making eye contact with me.

Unlike Nika, Rennoc made sure to meet my eyes as he walked away to join the girls. He did not speak, but the look he gave me was enough to tell me that he was with Lae, one hundred percent.

Poor Haras looked torn as he watched his

friends break apart. I felt a spark of hope. If anyone, Haras would stand by me … wouldn't he? Haras took a deep breath, as if preparing to say something, but then he decided against it. He met my eyes, and shook his head sadly. I felt like I was melting into the ground as I watched him run after the others.

With only Alyk remaining, I silently pleaded that he look me in the eye, but he stared at the ground in front of me instead.

"Please …" By this point I was very much regretting all the cruel things I'd said, and I was desperate for any support.

Then Alyk looked up and caught my gaze. It was only for a second, but just enough for me to see the determination and fear – deep fear – in his dark brown eyes. I knew right then that Alyk was hiding something – something important. He turned and ran before I could enquire.

Then I was alone.

My mother's fate was in my hands and I had no one to help me. It was up to me – and only me – to save her. I cannot even begin to describe how alone I felt.

My breath caught in my throat as it dawned on me. My friends had abandoned me, just as the mirror had shown.

If the mirror really contained the Seer's

talent, then the other horrible things would happen as well, I realized.

A sickening feeling arose in my stomach as I recalled the look of pure terror my mother would give as the dagger flew towards her heart.

And that man holding my necklace … it was Dennek.

I was shaking.

My knees buckled and my legs gave way. I collapsed to the ground and curled into a ball on my side. I pulled my hands and arms around my face and sobbed my heart out.

This was unfair.

I was only thirteen, too young to carry such a great weight on my shoulders. Everything was wrong. I wanted to go back in time to start over. To live my life without mad kings, cursed necklaces and creepy ghost people. I was only thirteen, too young to be making life-or-death decisions that most adults didn't have to contend with. Just yesterday morning I'd been living a normal life, my biggest decisions *what to wear to school*, and *how to deal with Mrs. Roy*. My life had changed so fast, all as a result of a simple ceremony gone wrong.

Why me?

I cried more than I ever had in my life, not caring who noticed me or what they would do when they did.

Slowly, I cried myself to sleep.

I awoke to a light tapping on my shoulder. I took my hands away from my face and opened my eyes. The sky was pitch black, and covered in thousands of tiny, glittering stars. I guessed it was just after midnight – approximately six hours until Dennek killed my mother.

I looked around for whatever had awakened me. To my left was the silvery figure of a girl. She was colorless and had no facial expression that I could read clearly. Now, at night, she seemed to be glowing, letting off a faint white light that lit up the ground around her.

I frowned. "Lia?"

Lia nodded slowly.

"What are you doing here?"

"I can help you."

Tilting my head to one side, I asked, "What do you mean?" I couldn't help but show my relief.

The whisp seemed to hesitate before replying, "Come with me." She gestured for me to follow her, and then started calmly walking away, without even waiting for me to stand up.

"Wait." I scrambled to my feet, and rushed after her. "Why are you helping me?"

Lia turned her head to look at me blankly, as always, but she did not answer.

"I mean ... *you* asked *us* for help ... and we failed you."

Lia shook her head. "I wouldn't accuse you of something deceptive without knowing what really happened."

Taken aback by her words, I grabbed Lia's shoulder, the force causing her to stop abruptly and twist towards me. "You're giving me another chance?"

She blinked. "Isn't that what friends do?"

I released her shoulder and we continued to walk through the silent village, unspeaking.

I guess I haven't been a very good friend then, I thought gloomily.

CHAPTER 10

THE IMPORTANCE OF FRIENDSHIP

Lia led me along the many rows of silent shops and houses, not stopping to tell me what was happening or even where she was taking me. After approximately ten minutes of blindly following her, immense curiosity got the better of me.

"Where are we going?" I asked.

Instead of answering, however, Lia simply turned her head just enough to make eye contact with me for a few seconds, then redirected her gaze to the dirt road in front of her.

Annoyed by the lack of information, I attempted – and failed – to conceal a groan. But if Lia had noticed, she gave no sign. I gave up pestering her for answers and started paying closer attention to the buildings around me.

Looking up at a second-storey window on my right, I could swear I saw a human-shaped shadow moving. I wondered what the non-whisps of Jesburgon would see if they looked out of their windows. They wouldn't be able to see Lia, but would they see a strange human-shaped light form wandering through their village, closely followed by a confused-looking girl?

We came to the edge of the more populated part of the village and Lia kept going. For the next twenty minutes or so, we walked past smaller clusters of houses, and farther out, several farms. It was around that time, when my whole body was burning with anticipation, that I asked Lia yet again where we were headed. Her response was the same.

Eventually, we came to what seemed to be an old, abandoned farm on the outskirts of Jesburgon. The wooden fences were rotting, the ancient looking barn desperately needed repairs, while the fields were congested with weeds and looked like they hadn't been trimmed in years. I also noticed a small flickering light – a fire most likely – beside a large run-down farmhouse a short distance away.

I was just about to ask another question – which would probably have been left unanswered – when someone called Lia's name from behind us, making me jump.

"Lia." I spun around. The speaker was a boy of around my age – another whisp. He had the same back-and-white appearance as Lia, but he also had his own distinctive look, just like any regular human.

"Mallie." Lia did not sound at all surprised to see the other whisp. Then again, I had never seen her show any emotions at all.

"Something has come up, Lia. You must come with me; it's urgent."

For most people, a phrase such as that would be very emotional for both the informer and the receiver. However, both whisps remained as calm and emotionless as ever. *What has Dennek done to these people?* I wondered.

"I'm sorry," Lia said, turning back to me. "Do you see that fire?" I nodded, looking at the small flickering light beside the farmhouse. "Go there; they can help you." I nodded again, not taking my eyes off the fire. I could now spot several figures around it.

"Thank you ..." Remembering my manners, I turned back to the two whisps, only to find that they were gone. I was alone once more.

Taking a deep breath to gather my courage, I started towards the fire. As I got closer, I noticed something familiar about the five figures sitting around it, but it wasn't until I was too close to turn back that I realized who they were.

Sitting around the fire were Haras, Lae, Nika, Alyk and Rennoc.

Why had Lia brought me here? Did she really think they would help me? After all the cruel things I'd said to them? Did Lia even know about that? She must have, or she would have told me where we were headed. She must have thought I'd refuse if I'd known, and she was correct. Even as I stood only twenty meters away, I was tempted to simply turn and run, and hope they didn't notice me.

Then I remembered Lia's words. *Second chances, isn't that what friends do?* Would they give me a second chance? Would I give me a second chance in their place?

"Lexa?" My stomach dropped as five pairs

of eyes suddenly snapped in my direction. I'd taken too long; fate had already made up its mind.

Taking a deep breath, I walked the rest of the way over to the fire.

"Look," I began. "I ... I'm sorry, I really am." No one replied, so I continued, more desperately this time. "I didn't mean anything I said earlier. I didn't ... I wasn't ..." Unsure of how to continue my apology, I ended up closing my mouth to choke back tears.

"No, *I'm* sorry." Confused, I looked at Lae, who was staring into the orange flames. She looked up at me, as if she could feel the heat of my gaze, and I saw that she had a dead serious expression on her face.

"I yelled at you," I said.

"Well, I kind of provoked it."

I was astonished. I'd never seen Lae as an apologetic person. I guess there was more to the small blonde than being a bossy leader.

"I was being selfish," she continued. "You were overcome by shock and grief, and I should have tried to see things from your perspective."

"The point is, Lexa, we've changed our minds," said Rennoc. "We were going to go find you."

"We will get your mother back, even if it

means handing over our necklaces," said Nika.

"Any mother of a friend is worth giving up an amazing talent for," Haras concluded.

I blinked back tears, wondering what in the world I had done to deserve these wonderful, forgiving people – my friends.

I just couldn't let them make that kind of sacrifice for me.

"No," I said. "I won't let you give up something you love so much for my cause."

Every one of my friends was stunned by my sudden decision.

"But … your mother …" Nika began.

"We'll do it another way," I said, as a sketchy plan began to take shape in my mind.

"What do you mean?" Rennoc asked curiously.

"We'll go to Lord Dennek, just as he expects us to, but we won't give him our necklaces. We'll use them *against* him instead," I declared, more confidently. I looked at each of them, nodding thoughtfully.

"That might actually work," Lae said. Then she noticed my watery eyes. "Don't start crying again," she begged.

Suddenly, all of my bad feelings for Lae sprinted away, leaving only good, warm ones. She was going to help me rescue my mother, no matter how crazy my plan was. For that, I was very grateful. I plopped down beside my friend and threw my arms around her, squeezing hard.

Lae's muscles tightened in surprise. She pulled away from me, a look of discomfort on her face.

"What's wrong?" I asked in concern.

"I just …" Lae kept switching her gaze, looking everywhere but back at me. "I've … never been hugged before," she admitted finally.

How could anyone live without being hugged? Without being loved? Lae had never mentioned her life before we met, and to be truthful, I'd never really wondered about it. Perhaps it had not been as happy and loving as mine. Perhaps that was why she hadn't originally seen rescuing my mother as a top priority.

"Well, there's always a first time," I told Lae softly. She didn't answer, which was quite unlike her.

I cautiously placed my arms back around her chest. She flinched when I touched her, but this time she didn't pull away. After a few long, awkward seconds, Lae reached over and placed her arms around me in return. It wasn't passionate, but it was a first.

Rennoc cleared his throat and Lae and I broke apart.

"We only have a few more hours before dawn," he reminded us.

My heart rate sped up. We would have to leave now.

"Right. So, which way to Lord Dennek's castle?" I asked whomever.

"There's a path that goes through those woods," said Alyk, pointing to the tall, ominous trees behind us.

Haras stood up briskly. "Let's go get Lexa's mother back!" he said.

CHAPTER 11

INTO THE DRAGON'S LAIR

"Why is Dennek's castle in the middle of the woods?" I asked.

"Probably to keep out unimportant visitors," Rennoc said.

"I'd imagine it works then."

The woods that surrounded the path to Lord Dennek's castle were indeed very intimidating. There was something about this particular forest that made me feel uneasy – a different kind of 'uneasy' from when we had walked to Mencia and back again. Even Nika and Lae, who normally loved the woods – and nature in general – were quiet and jumpy.

Around ten minutes in, I glanced over my

shoulder for the umpteenth time, to see a pair of blood-red eyes staring back at me from the shadows of the tall trees. Unable to contain the massive wave of alarm rushing over me, I let out a loud, high-pitched scream and squeezed my eyes shut.

I could almost feel the panic sweeping over the group. At the sound of my scream, my friends jolted to a stop, more alert than ever. A couple – namely Alyk and Nika – yelped in surprise. We waited in silent anticipation for a few seconds that seemed like an eternity, for something to happen.

"What?" Rennoc asked, almost angrily. I gathered the courage to look back at where I'd seen the creature. Naturally, it had disappeared.

"There was … a pair of eyes, over there." I pointed. We all stared into the shadows for another few seconds.

"I don't see anything," said Haras eventually.

"It was probably just your imagination playing tricks on you," Lae said, but she didn't seem convinced.

In total, we walked along for maybe a quarter of an hour, twisting and turning with the winding path through that dark, menacing forest, until we caught our first glimpse of the castle. It was big, but not massive – maybe three quarters the size of King Trub's castle in Mencia. A large stone wall circled the building, the only opening being directly in line with the path, guarded by a tough-looking sentry with a sword at his hip. I shuddered, imagining what it was meant to keep out.

"So, we just walk right through the gates?" asked Nika, already doubting my plan.

"Of course," I said defiantly, although my stomach was churning with anxiety and my hands felt tingly.

"Like Lexa said, Dennek is expecting us to give up," Lae said, "so he'll have told his guard to look out for us." I was grateful to her for supporting my plan with such conviction. I *really* hoped she was right.

We approached the gates slowly. Coincidentally – or quite possibly not – I recognized the guard at the gate. It was Winel, who'd picked us up from the Jesburgon train station. I remembered how a young messenger – Locky, I believe his name was – had saved us from the intimidating man's clutches by coming to tell Winel that 'the boss' needed him. Their boss, I now understood, was Lord Dennek.

As we neared the large man, he narrowed his eyes, and a wicked grin crept onto his face.

"So it *is* you." I swallowed hard.

We came to a stop in a tightly knit group before Winel, who checked us over – presumably looking for any types of weapons – then continued. "Come with me, the Lord will see you soon."

With that, Winel turned his back to us, then he strode through the gates and up the stone steps to the big wooden doors of the castle, leaving us to scramble warily behind him.

I looked over my shoulder one last time, to see the gates in the wall closing silently behind us, as if by magic.

Though the castle was smaller – therefore less impressive – than King Trub's, the interior decoration was grand. Crystal chandeliers hung from the ceiling. Large landscape paintings, portraits and everything in between decorated the walls of the corridors to my left and right. A long spiral staircase located in a corner of the huge entrance hall led up to more floors of this amazing space. Spread out across the floor was an immense rug of deep purple with *Jesburgon* stitched neatly in large silver letters.

Dennek certainly had a taste for expensive furnishings.

"Whoa," said Rennoc softly, expressing my sentiments exactly.

We followed Winel down one of the corridors leading out of the entrance hall. None of the doorways positioned every twenty steps or so had any actual doors in them, so I was able to discreetly peer through each one, as we passed. Most of the rooms were packed with shelves full of pretty random stuff that you'd normally just see sitting around a house – well, some rich person's house. An expensive looking pair of yellow running shoes, a fury brown hat, a pair of large glasses with lenses that were black as ice caught my eye.

One of the rooms appeared to be empty except for a stand in the center of the room with a strange golden coin sitting on top. Another looked just like an office – or maybe an interrogation room. It held a single big black desk with chairs on either side. Stacks of papers blocked my view of the chair farthest away from me.

As we neared the end of the corridor, I began to wonder which of the remaining doorways we would be going through, but that question became prominent as the last doorway came into view. This one *did* have a door in its frame, and a heavy-looking metal one at that. If Lord Dennek were keeping a prisoner anywhere, it would probably be through there.

We reached the door and Winel removed a skinny metal cylinder from one of his jacket's pockets, which he slid through a circular hole just above the doorknob. I heard a faint click, before Winel pushed open the now unlocked door and led us down the steps on the other side. I followed apprehensively, knowing that every step took me closer to Lord Dennek – and hopefully, to my mother.

Hearing a loud *slam* behind me, I gasped and whipped my head around in alarm. The metal door had closed – seemingly by itself – after Alyk, the last of our group, had come through. My hands shaking, I cautiously turned back to follow Winel down the hallway of this basement part of the castle. I couldn't help noticing that each closing door trapped us deeper inside the dragon's lair.

This corridor was very similar to the one upstairs – with one distinct difference. A locked metal door, not unlike the one we'd come through initially, guarded each room. I wondered what secrets Dennek was hiding behind those doors. Then again, perhaps I didn't want to know.

Winel came to a stop at one of the doors, which – at least to me – seemed no different from any of the others. He inserted another small cylinder rod, and pushed open the door for us.

"In you go," he said, rather unkindly. The six of us piled in, staying as close as possible to one another, and stood as a group facing Winel as he slammed the door on us, blocking our exit. Not a word was spoken.

Turning slightly to my right, the first thing that caught my eye was the wall on that side – or rather what was painted on it. From what I could tell, the mural was made up of a variety of smaller scenes, most of which contained at least one of the same five people. Five people who looked somewhat ... familiar. I took a step out of the safety of our close group to examine it further.

"Lexa?" I froze in my tracks at the desperate, yet hopeful voice I knew so well. Quickly spinning around, I gasped.

"Mum!" On the opposite side of the nearly empty room was a birdcage – the largest I'd ever seen. And there stood my mother, face pressed up against the thick bars of her prison, her beautiful ocean-blue eyes bright with fear.

I took a few steps towards her; slow at first, as I still could barely believe whom I was seeing, but faster as I grew closer. My mother's smile widened, but quickly faded, as she seemed to realize something.

"Wait, you ..." She was cut off instantly.

Because all of a sudden, he was there. Lord Dennek appeared out of thin air, blocking me from making contact with my mother. I inhaled sharply and skidded to a stop, my first emotion being fear. Then it dawned on me that this was the man who'd caused me so much pain. This was the man who'd kidnapped my mother, and wanted my necklace in return. I was going to make him pay, but first things first ...

"Give me my mother." I spoke forcefully, showing no sign of my previous fear.

Lord Dennek raised his eyebrows. "Ah, well, you haven't completed your part of the deal, so ..."

"I'm not here to give up my necklace!" I screeched, realizing too late that I had just ruined our plan of a surprise attack. Dennek didn't even flinch. In fact, he did quite the opposite.

"Well then, what are you going to exchange for your mother?" He smiled smugly, almost teasing me. I scowled in return.

Dennek made a show of craning his neck to see behind me. "*Their* necklaces then? I see you've brought them with you. Good, good."

"I would never betray my friends," I

countered.

Lord Dennek just grinned mischievously. "Oh really? Well, your *friends* seem to think differently. Why, even quiet little Alyk has betrayed *all* of you."

Taken aback, I didn't respond immediately. Alyk? The shy boy who'd stayed in the shadows of our group had betrayed us? He would never. Or would he? I thought back to the woods, and how Alyk had disappeared when the rest of us weren't looking.

"No," Nika said. "Alyk *is* our friend. He wouldn't betray us." But even she sounded unsure.

I turned my back to Dennek, and looked at my friends. They'd moved closer to me during the exchange, and were now standing in a sloppy line, or a lopsided semicircle. Alyk had turned pale, looking as colorless as a whisp.

Before I knew what was happening, Lord Dennek threw some kind of sparkling black dust over Alyk. It trickled down his body like water, all flowing to a particular area on the tile floor in front of all of us. As it swirled around, certain parts changed colour – just like the water in the pond when Lord Dennek's face appeared – and soon we were looking at Alyk's face in the strange black dust.

He seemed to be in mid conversation with someone. "She lives in the village of Kaprota, in Mencia. I know it's the smallest village, so it shouldn't be too hard to track her from there." My heart skipped a beat. He was talking about *my* village. There was a bit of silence as Alyk listened to whomever he was having his conversation with. "Oh yeah, she loves her too much for her own good. I can pretty much guarantee she'll do anything for her. Girl breaks down just thinking about being away from her mommy." Alyk paused to roll his eyes and my blood went cold.

No, it couldn't be.

"And don't forget about your part of the deal. I want one of those precious necklaces you're after," Alyk spoke again.

My breathing became unsteady. This couldn't be happening. *Dennek is tricking us*, I thought.

"Nice doing business with you my lord," Alyk finished, and the black dust dissolved into nothing.

There was one thing on my mind. Alyk was a traitor. He was working for Dennek.

CHAPTER 12

FATE

Alyk's fault ... Alyk's fault ... the words played over and over in my mind like a heartbeat. Alyk was the reason my mother was about to be murdered.

I was brought back to my senses by a sudden sharp pain around my neck. I stumbled backwards, my hands coming up to my throat instinctively. I felt a cold metal chain under my fingertips and horror struck as I realized what was trying to choke me. My necklace was being pulled back by its pendant, harder now, harder still.

I couldn't breathe. Pure panic settled in.

I tried to grab at the chain, to pry it off, but

my efforts were useless against the tightening force causing my necklace to dig into my throat.

Tears of desperation escaped from my eyes. I tried to cry out in pain, but all that came out was a small squeak. Even that wasted most of my leftover breath.

My vision was becoming blurry, and my thoughts, clouded. The panic intensified, for I knew I was losing air.

The world was spinning around me. Everything seemed too confusing. My only clear thought was that I desperately needed to breathe. I collapsed backwards onto the floor.

"Lexa!" In the back of my mind, I heard my name being called, by whom I wasn't sure. I couldn't focus on anything at that moment.

Lying on my back made it no easier to breathe, and it made the pain worse. The chain was slowly making its way to the top of my neck, just under my chin, digging into the flesh and pulling harder than ever. Wherever it had already cut my neck stung like it was on fire, and I could feel warm droplets of blood forming.

Blackness threatened to take over, and it took every ounce of my energy and concentration to avoid it. I knew Lord Dennek wanted my necklace, and I knew that necklace was the most precious thing I owned, but at that moment I wanted nothing more than to let him have it.

Just let me breathe, I thought. *Take away the pain.*

As if fate had heard my silent plea, the chain finally slipped off my neck.

I gasped for breath, taking in as much air as I could before having to breathe out again.

I lay there, sprawled on the floor with my eyes squeezed shut, panting and coughing. My lungs ached from lack of air, and my neck and chin stung like I'd never experienced before. I brought my hand up to my throat, and found it wet with blood. Other than that however, I seemed fine.

Satisfied that I wasn't about to drop dead from major injuries or anything of the sort, I allowed myself to take in my surroundings once more.

I could hear Dennek laughing like a madman behind me. A feeling of dread replaced my sense of relief. Lord Dennek had my necklace now, and there was nothing I could do about it.

I rolled over onto my hands and knees, and stood up slowly, turning to face my enemy. Dangling from his open palm was my necklace. I recognized the scene from Trub's mirror immediately. The mirror had been right twice now, and there was only one more thing that was supposed to happen – the one I dreaded most.

Then I saw that there were already four other necklaces with different coloured pendants around the evil lord's neck. Scorching red, cloudy grey, fawn brown, and spring green. Somehow Dennek had pulled the necklaces off each of us.

Lord Dennek's cold black eyes glinted triumphantly. "You fools! Did you really believe you could outsmart the lord of Jesburgon? You must have known I'd have a backup plan." Lord Dennek laughed out loud. He slipped a leather glove off the hand that was not being used to hold my necklace and tucked it into a pouch at his hip. "Telekinesis can be a very useful talent, wouldn't you agree?" He smiled mysteriously.

Telekinesis – that must have been how he'd gotten the necklaces to come to him. But then, was Dennek's glove like the mirror? Did it contain the telekinetic talent?

"Now I am the one to possess all five legendary talents." I watched helplessly as Dennek slipped the remaining necklace over his head.

I held my breath and waited. A second

passed, then two, then five. An undoubtedly confused expression crept onto the lord's face. He looked down expectantly at the five necklaces sitting innocently around his neck. I was not entirely sure what we were waiting for, probably something like what happened on the train.

The train ...

Something clicked into place in the back of my mind and the gears started turning. My jumbled thoughts began fitting together like puzzle pieces, creating a clear image.

Back on the train, I now remembered, our necklaces had glowed and buzzed, but only when Haras had shown up, because they'd sensed each other's presence. Then the necklaces had all connected. I recalled a brilliant flash of strange light, and a ball of aqua-blue splashing over my head, filling a part of me that I hadn't known was empty.

Water wasn't my *necklace's* talent, it was mine. My necklace had transferred it into me back on the train, just as my friends' necklaces had done to them. Therefore, Lord Dennek could not take over any of our talents because they were now well and truly *our* talents.

I smiled as my hope returned.

"What?" snapped Lord Dennek. "You find this funny?"

I crossed my arms and proudly announced my discovery.

"The necklaces don't have their talents anymore. They've already transferred them to *us*," I told him.

Only a few minutes ago, Dennek had been so smug and sure of himself. Now, seeing him in this state of confusion and disbelief, I almost felt sorry for him. *Almost.*

"You can't have these *legendary* talents because *we* already have them," I finished, satisfied that I'd made the lord feel like an idiot.

I watched Dennek's eyes narrow, his forehead scrunching together, as he slowly realized what my words meant. His face went red; his jaw contorted into a horrible position that made him look like he was about bite something … or someone. His hands balled into tights fists that looked ready to punch the living daylights out of me.

I didn't think I'd seen anyone so furious. Once again, I felt fear rise in the pit of my stomach.

Without warning, the enraged lord cried out in anger, as he ripped all five necklaces off and smashed them onto the tile floor with such force that I couldn't help but gasp and pray that my enchanting aqua jewel had not broken.

He looked me directly in the eyes. "You know what this means, don't you?"

Before I could process what he was saying, the lord swiftly drew a silver dagger. He then aimed with deadly precision, and threw it – directly at my mother's heart.

I could only watch in horror as the dagger soared across the room.

There was a blur of movement, and suddenly Alyk was in the dagger's path. It hit him square in the chest and he staggered backwards with the impact. The boy had just enough time to make eye contact with me, and I could see the clear apology in his dark eyes, before they became unfocussed and he crumpled to the floor.

He was surely dead.

CHAPTER 13

ELEMENTAL POWER

I was stunned. For the first few moments my feet seemed frozen in place and I could only gape at the body of the boy I'd only minutes ago thought of as a lying traitor. Yet there he was, sprawled on the floor at the foot of my mother's cage because he'd taken the dagger – the one that had haunted my thoughts – for her. He was no more a traitor than he was a hero. Her saviour.

I scrambled over to the crumpled body. Alyk was on his side, his top arm hanging limply across his chest, blocking my view of the wound. I took his shoulder and rolled him over onto his back, and his arm flopped to the floor on his other side, leaving me a clear view of the silver dagger embedded in his flesh.

My hands automatically cupped over my mouth at the sight. Tears filled my eyes as I realized the hopelessness of the situation. Around the dagger – still standing vertically – a splotch of dark blood soaked through his once nice-looking cotton shirt, slowly but surely getting larger as more blood oozed from the wound.

A tear escaped my watery eyes. I felt it trickle down the side of my face and drip off my chin.

I remembered Alyk's aloofness, and his confusing expressions. What if it had had something to do with his betrayal? What if it was something he couldn't control? Maybe it was important, even threatening. I cursed myself for not saying anything on the matter. It wasn't fair. Nothing was truly fair in the world. Especially the mere existence of a certain lord.

"You're a monster." I continued to stare at Alyk, not looking back at Dennek until a moment after I'd spoken. The lord had begun moving towards the exit while all eyes were on Alyk's body. "Where are you going?" He froze, with his back towards me, only a few floor tiles from escaping.

"What do you want?" he asked through gritted teeth, still unmoving.

I rose slowly from my friend's side. My insides started churning with hatred. "I want? Isn't it always what *you* want, you greedy, despicable, fraud!" It felt surprisingly good to spit out all my negative thoughts. "But since you asked, yeah, there is a thing or two that I want from you. I want my mother back, I want my friend back, and I want all those poor whisps turned back into humans. And most of all, I want you *gone*."

An uncomfortable silence followed. Dennek was still facing the door, so I could not get a good look at his face, but I did hear his discrete sigh of defeat, and triumph flickered in my chest.

All of a sudden, he lunged for the door, banging it open before I could move. But I didn't need to move, because the metal door slammed shut again with a startling *bang*, pushing Dennek back with enormous force.

"You're not going anywhere." I heard Rennoc's voice and silently praised him for being on the alert.

Dennek turned around to face us, his eyes narrowed. "Fine, let it be this way then."

His concentration not breaking, Dennek's hand crept down to the leather pouch on his hip. Opening the flap, he pulled out a small circular object, which he held up in front of himself. I nearly raised my eyebrows, and then decided against it. With Dennek and his tricks, I wouldn't be able to know if this was really just a pathetic attempt to protect himself.

At least we still had our talents. My mother was still alive. My plan hadn't failed yet, and I couldn't let Alyk's sacrifice go to waste.

A floor tile at Dennek's feet cracked, and burst into the air, leaving a small space for a thick vine to come through. Growing taller, the vine twisted its way around Dennek as a second exploded up from his other side. Dennek seemed to decide that now was the time to act, and thrust his circular thing at the first vine. To my astonishment, it expanded quickly, transforming into a large, steel shield. The vine did not even touch the shield; it recoiled hastily as it expanded to full size. The second vine, however, sneakily wound its way around Dennek's forearm while his attention was on the first, and squeezed tightly. But the lord swung his shield around to his other side. The vine didn't back away fast enough, and there was a nasty hissing as the metal connected with the plant. Then it started to crumble. Starting where it had been touched, the vine withered away, turning into dust, spreading like a disease.

Lae let out a high-pitched squeak as her plant crumbled to the ground. I turned my head to give her a sympathetic look, but my eye caught Nika instead. The girl had her eyes closed, and her head tilted ever so slightly towards the ceiling. Her hands were pulled into fists, like someone who's concentrating very hard, and she seemed to be muttering something over and over. I was about to look back at Dennek when she opened her eyes, a look of hope etched on her face.

A series of gasps caused me to look in the other direction again. A black bear had appeared in the space that separated us from Dennek.

A ball of fire flew through the air towards Dennek. Blazing with bright orange light, and rotating like a regular throwing ball from my village, it looked like a small sun. Dennek saw the fireball, and brought his shield up to expertly block it. As the two connected, time seemed to freeze. At first, the fireball brightened, and I began to have hope that maybe this magic shield was not immune to fire, but then it flickered and went out. Rather than turning to dust like the vine, it simply disappeared.

I doubt anyone had time to process what

had just happened, because then the bear roared loudly, before stomping towards Dennek. It reared up on its back legs to stand at full height – a great deal higher than Dennek – and roared again. With droplets of saliva flying out onto everything in the area, its mouth opened so wide that it could have chomped Dennek's head off in an instant.

For the first time, Lord Dennek began to look a little panicked. He constantly shifted his gaze from the malicious vine to the dangerous bear and back again, anticipating an attack from either.

Another fireball soared towards its target, and I felt the heat on my side for a split second as it passed. This time, distracted by two opponents, Dennek barely managed to deflect it. The glowing ball of fire hit the edge of his shield and veered off towards the left before flickering out as before. There was just enough time for the vine to strike him across his neck while his back was turned, and he cried out in pain and rage. The bear chose that moment to take its first act of offence, and swiped its paw at Dennek's shoulder. The man cried out a second time as the sharp claws tore through his jacket, leaving deep gashes and drawing blood.

To defend himself, Dennek thrust his

shield in the direction of the more threatening attacker. Just like the vine, the bear seemed to sense the damage that the magic shield could inflict. It recoiled as quickly as it could on its back legs and its front paws flumped down. Spotting the opportunity with the bear's hasty retreat, Dennek took a few tentative steps towards the animal, his shield held up. The bear growled a warning, but kept moving backwards, out of the shield's reach.

Then Dennek jerked backwards, as if pulled by some invisible force. He stumbled, trying to regain his balance. His arms flailing, he nearly lost his grip on his only weapon. I recognized the action; it was the one of a person fighting a strong wind.

The lord's feet started sliding back against his will, he howled in outrage. The vine snaked its way through the air and wrapped itself around Dennek's ankle, helping to corner him once again.

That's about the time when it dawned on me that my friends were all making their best efforts to beat Dennek, while I stood around watching, being completely useless. And this had been my idea in the first place. *Water, water, water,* I thought, glancing around the room. But alas, no pool of water had magically appeared since I'd entered – not that I had expected it to. Still, I cursed under my breath. How else was I supposed to help?

Until now, I had only been able to manipulate water, unlike Haras, who could create fire. Actually, I'd never even tried to create water. Perhaps it was possible. Or maybe I could summon it from elsewhere, like I guessed Nika had done.

I looked down at my hands, concentrating on my task. I closed my eyes calmly and searched my body for where my talent was stored. I imagined rummaging through a chest full of superfluous items – not unlike the stuff in Dennek's storerooms – for something direly needed.

"No!"

My eyes snapped open instantaneously, just as Nika hurried over to her bear, which was stumbling away from Dennek, obviously in pain. From where I was standing, I could see the tears glistening in her eyes as she placed her two hands on the bear's snout. My insides jerked. The shield had hit the bear. He was crumbling, like the vine. Tweep scampered up Nika's side and stopped on her forearm to look at her. The girl seemed to understand what the little squirrel was saying to her. She nodded as the tears began to fall.

Tweep jumped down from her arm and

scampered over to the lord, taking the bear's place as Nika's animal champion. He pounced on Dennek's shoe, scratching ferociously, but did little damage. Dennek just seemed to think of him as a nuisance. He simply shook his foot hard and Tweep fell to the ground. But although he was small, the squirrel was very determined, and he got right back up to try to take down Dennek, squirrel-style.

Another ball of fire came soaring towards Dennek, and this time, the lord was ready – or so he thought. Midway, the fireball gained speed, as if being pushed by something – wind. In the second that the two elements connected, they kind of mixed together, to create a swirling ball of red and silver light. And this time, when it hit Dennek's shield, it made impact. Pushing Dennek back towards the vine, which grabbed hold of him, wrapping twice around his waist.

The swirling ball of light bounced off the shield ... and came hurtling towards me. I dropped to my stomach so fast that even the athletic kids in my village would have been impressed. Even though it was supposed to be on our side, I had no idea what the ball was capable of. I didn't want to take any chances.

Getting back on my feet, I noticed

something that made my heart soar. Dennek's shield was dented where the light had hit it. Maybe there was a weakness. Maybe there was a path to victory.

I remembered Lae's words from the night before. *Think of all the terrible things he could do with the power of all the elements*, she'd said. *What damage could they cause when used together?*

All the elements …

Then the solution hit me. "Together! We have to combine the elements!" I shouted, not really caring that Dennek could also hear every word I said. Because what could he do, against such power. I'd seen what happened with two elements. What about all five?

A burst of light caused me to look quickly over to my right, where the boys were standing so close together that they were almost touching. As a result, they had managed to recreate what they had accidentally done before. With a flick of his wrist, Haras sent it flying at Dennek. Except it didn't work out exactly as he'd expected it to. Instead of a ball, it split into two coloured beams of light, each coming from one of their hands.

Like a laser, each beam shot across the room, not breaking from a straight line until meeting something solid – Dennek. He yelped in pain as the silver beam of light hit him in the back. Smoke started to pour from the spot, and he swung his shield around for protection in a panic, slicing the vine in his confusion. Lae grunted in fury as her remaining vine turned to dust.

A third beam of light – this one green – shot from her outstretched hand. As it touched the metal shield, along with the others, a thin crack appeared, slowly elongating to the length of the shield. Dennek's eyes squeezed shut, his face twisted in pain from the strain.

A forth beam of light joined the first three. Nika still had one hand on the bear's snout – her touch seemed to put a pause to the process of turning to dust – but she used her other hand to direct her beam of warm brown light in Dennek's direction. Increasing the crack in the shield.

Now there was just me. Our victory lay in my ability to use my talent without any actual water.

Taking a deep breath that I blew out audibly through my lips, I closed my eyes and focussed more than I ever had.

This time, instead of searching my body, I went deep into my soul. The symbolic objects in this chest were nowhere near as useless.

Each was valuable to my personality, my spirit. Each helped make up who I was as a person. A friendly, emotional, determined person. And that was where I discovered my talent. A well of endless water.

I imagined sending a bucket down the well, and then I reeled it back up, full to the top with water. I felt a cold tingling run down the veins in my right arm to my fingertips. I smiled.

Opening my eyes, I reached out with my palm aimed at Dennek. A thick laser beam of aqua-blue light shot out to join the other four elements.

The shield snapped in two and the pieces clattered to the floor.

With no protection left, Dennek howled in pain as the power of all five elements hit him. His body began to smoke.

But the lord had one more trick up his sleeve. Literally.

In one swift motion, Dennek drew a small golden coin from the cuff of his jacket and threw it onto the floor at his feet.

He disappeared in a flash of light and a crack like thunder.

CHAPTER 14

ALYK

I knew we hadn't defeated Lord Dennek, but I did not feel disappointed, knowing he was still alive. He was gone, at least for now, and I was able to free my mother.

I stood there for a few seconds, staring at the spot where Dennek had been only moments ago, my mind spinning with facts, lies and questions.

I turned around, still processing the past half hour or so, and there was my mother. Standing at the bars of her cage, gazing in awe. At the sight of the woman who I always believed would protect me, the woman I loved more than anyone else in the world, all of my emotions came pouring back into my shocked, emotionless body. I wanted nothing more than to be with her again, and now, Dennek wasn't around to stop me.

I rushed to the man-sized birdcage, barely slowing to squeeze my arms between the bars and wrap my arms around my mother's torso. I felt warm relief as she did the same. I felt her soothing fingers stroke through my hair, and her hand on the back of my head as she pulled me closer.

Everything would be all right.

"You have a lot to tell me," she whispered into my ear.

"I do, and I *will* tell you. Every little detail," I promised in return. I pulled away, just enough to look up into her aqua blue eyes. "First, we have to get you out of here."

A whisper from behind me, however, completely changed my priorities.

"He's still alive."

I spun around to see my friends gathered around Alyk. Nika had his wrist in her hand, two fingers feeling for a pulse.

Rennoc narrowed his eyes in disbelief. "He can't be."

I broke away from my mother and went slowly over to Alyk. It was almost too much. His shirt was now soaked in his own blood, and his skin was deathly pale.

"Are you sure?" I asked. I didn't want Alyk to be dead, but I really couldn't see how he could still be alive. I knelt down on the floor between Rennoc and Lae and gently picked up his other wrist, feeling around with my fingers for a pulse. For a few panicky moments, I felt nothing. Then there was the soft thud of a heartbeat. A burst of joy filled my upper body. "He's still alive!"

"I wouldn't be too happy," Lae said. "Unless we get help immediately, he'll die anyway." Sometimes I hated Lae for being so realistic, although she did have a point.

"Then why are we all just sitting here? We have to go find a healer!" I cried urgently.

"Lae just shook her head sadly. "We're in Jesburgon, remember?" The village for the *untalented*?"

"There must be *someone* with a healing talent; how else could they care for the sick and injured?" Rennoc said.

"Weren't there other ways? I mean, before the Globe of Tarahabi, our ancestors used herbs or something. Maybe the untalented still do?" Haras suggested, thinking deeply. "Lae! Lae can grow herbs, can't you Lae?"

"Guys," Nika shushed us. Then in the silence, I heard it, a low humming from the other side of the room. A sense of déjà vu came over me. I spun around to find the source.

The necklaces, still lying abandoned on the floor at varying distances, were glowing and vibrating.

The two closest to each other – red and green – snapped together, as if drawn by a strong magnetic force. Quickly, the others connected as well, and the glow brightened until the light was so intense that I was forced to squint. At the same time, the colours went down, each fading to a bright white.

Then I watched in awe and wonder, as the combined necklaces levitated off the floor and, hovering a few feet in the air, began to float in our direction, closer, and closer still. With each passing second, my curiosity grew.

Heading in my direction, the five glowing necklaces did not seem to have any intention of stopping. I scooted backwards to let them pass, and they continued along their path, before stopping to hover above Alyk's chest.

As one, the necklaces began to change colour again. Soon, they each glowed a relaxing violet colour.

Like a raindrop, the violet colour dropped down and splatted onto Alyk, just above his heart, leaving the jewels completely white.

The violet dissolved into his skin.

The magic over, the necklaces blinked back to normal and fell. Aided by his quick reflexes, Rennoc's hand darted out to catch them, managing all but mine. I tentatively reached out to pick it off Alyk's bloodied chest.

Without warning, the silver dagger unwedged itself from Alyk's flesh and clattered to the floor, the sudden movement causing me to grab my necklace and pull it towards my hurriedly.

No one spoke or moved.

Suddenly, Alyk gasped for air, and began breathing heavily. My friend's eyes fluttered open and darted around in confusion. I couldn't help but cry out. "Alyk!"

The very much alive boy looked instinctively in the direction of his name. Focusing on me, his dark eyes widened with recognition and guilt, filling with tears.

"Lexa," he choked. "I'm so sorry. I swear it wasn't me. I don't know how to explain it, but …" He grimaced. "There's something wrong with me."

I couldn't think of a reassuring answer – how does one respond to an apology like that? – so I remained silent.

Alyk's eyes moved down to focus on my

neck. "You're hurt."

I reached up to touch the cuts on my neck, which stung ferociously, causing me to wince. I could still feel the marks that the chain had made when it had dug into my skin, and sticky dried blood covered the scratches. "I'll be fine." I reassured Alyk.

Alyk ignored me. He slid his elbows back and pushed himself into a sitting position. Nika bolted forward to help him, but then retracted awkwardly when he shot her a look that clearly said, *I'm fine.*

He reached tentatively towards my neck with his right hand. I did not know what his intentions were, but I trusted him not to injure me further, at least not on purpose. After all, he'd said it hadn't been him who had betrayed us, and somehow I believed him. I tensed as his fingertips made contact with my skin, expecting more stinging, but instead I felt a warm, relieving sensation creep over my throat. I immediately felt peaceful and drowsy. I had no desire whatsoever for Alyk to remove his hand; in fact, I would have gladly stayed in that state for the rest of my life. So I felt somewhat disappointed when he finally did.

I sighed longingly, after coming out of my personal peace, and opened my eyes – though

I didn't recall closing them – to see the rest of my friends gaping at my throat.

"How ..." Rennoc began, but didn't seem to know how to finish.

I reached up to my neck again, questioning what everyone was so baffled by. My eyes widened. It no longer stung. I traced a finger along the cuts covering my throat, except they weren't there. The dried blood remained, but other than that I was entirely healed. I looked back at Alyk, dumbfounded. He at least seemed calm, if a bit confused.

"Healing," said Lae softly. "You have a healing talent."

"But ... I'm untalented."

I shook my head and shrugged. "I guess not."

There was a silence, as we were all lost in thought.

"Right," Lae said in her authoritative voice. "We should get out of here before Dennek comes back with reinforcements." She got briskly to her feet and strode over to my mother's cage. "How does this thing open. Do we need a key?"

I stood up, and joined Lae. "I can't see a keyhole. Or a lock for that matter," I said.

Behind me, I could hear the rest of the group getting to their feet. "I'll go see if the door is locked." I heard Haras say. Alyk came up beside me, examining the cage for an opening. I noticed my mother having a hard time averting her gaze from his bloodied shirt. I couldn't blame her.

"I'm sorry, I couldn't tell you how to open it. I must have been unconscious when that man left me in here." my mother said, rather unhelpfully.

"We'll find a way." I told her doubtfully.

"Guys."

I turned around to see Haras staring at the wall on the other side of the room – not just any wall, I realized, but the same one that I'd noticed upon entering, painted with a mural.

I crossed the room in several long strides. Those five people that the mural seemed to focus on, they certainly did look familiar. Especially the girl in the scene I was looking at.

She was standing about knee-deep in the ocean, watching the waves crashing in the distance. Her long, wavy, chocolate-brown hair blew freely in the ocean breeze. She had a long silver chain around her neck, from which a single blue pendant hung like a teardrop.

"Guys," I said, "I think this is ... *us.*"

EPILOGUE

Mira trudged along the empty dirt road, kicking stray rocks and staring down at the ground in front of her, oblivious to the happenings around her. She needn't pay attention anyhow, having traveled the path to Bya's small house many times in the past few days.

The girl blew a strand of her bright orange hair out of her face, but the action did little. The annoying strand of hair simply fell right back into its place – directly in front of her line of vision. She grunted in irritation, finally resorting to removing one hand from the large stack of old history books she was carrying, to tuck the strand of hair back behind her ear. *Everything would be so much better if Lexa were still here,* she thought miserably for the hundredth time.

Mira's life had changed considerably since that morning of her Talent Gaining. She could still remember it clearly. Lexa, who came before her in alphabetical order, had entered the auditorium, but unlike those before her, she had never exited.

Mira remembered the long, uncomfortable wait after the auditorium door had closed behind her friend. With each second, she'd gotten more anxious. No one's Talent Gaining took that long, something must have gone wrong. Then finally, after fifty million hours, the door had reopened, but to her great dismay, it was not Lexa who had stepped out.

The school director had whispered something in Mrs. Roy's ear, and her teacher's lips had pinched together – an expression Mira had yet to match to an emotion – at this news. As the director had disappeared back through the doorway, Mrs. Roy had gestured for Aluji to follow. And then Mira had been first in line.

After that, everything had happened in a blur. The Globe of Tarahabi had declared her a Seer, eliciting a slightly more enthusiastic round of applause than that for the other students. Seers were important to Mencia, and well respected by the citizens. There were a number of congratulations at the reception after the ceremony, and then, free for the remainder of the day, she went home. Only to be told the terrible truth of Lexa's weird disappearance by her concerned parents.

Her best friend was untalented. Mira would never see her again.

It was like a piece had fallen from her soul. The two girls had been best friends for as long as she could remember. Now that she was simply ... gone, Mira saw no reason to continue being the happy ray of sunshine that most people had come to recognize her as.

The worst part was that everyone in the village just continued on with their lives as if Lexa had never existed in the first place. The only other person who seemed to feel the loss was Mrs. Foote, Lexa's mother. Now that she thought of it, Mira hadn't seen Mrs. Foote in the past day or so.

While the rest of her classmates continued to attend school, Mira's education had been taken over by the village Seer herself. Bya was kind and wise, if a bit old – well, a lot old actually. No one in the village had become a Seer in many years. For so long, there had only been Bya to see into the ominous darkness that was the future. Now there was also Mira.

Her visions had started the very first day her training had begun. She had just about reached the small stone steps leading up to Bya's front door, when suddenly a scene flashed before her eyes. It wasn't huge, just of a large spider sitting in its newly made web in the frame of Bya's kitchen window. But it had shocked her, especially when she turned her head and there was a *real* spider, sitting its web in Bya's *real* kitchen window. After much reassuring from the senior Seer that it was completely normal, Mira had finally calmed down and accepted her role as a young Seer.

More visions came. Bya dropping a plate, her mother baking a pie, Aleine waving friendly on her way home. They all had little, if any, importance.

Until now.

Mira rounded a corner and started down the final path to Bya's house. All of a sudden, her thoughts were obscured by a flash of another vision. An obviously terrified girl, in the center of a dark room, her head darting around, searching for the danger hiding in the shadows. Then there was a pair of blood red eyes behind her, and something – a horrible creature – sprung out at the girl with its claws outstretched.

Returning to the present, Mira gasped and

dropped her books. She knew exactly who the girl was.

"Lexa!" she squeaked.

ABOUT THE AUTHOR

Alexa Wilcox began writing Aqua Jewel at the age of twelve, as a Christmas gift for her mother. She is passionate about books, a joy that she shares with her two sisters, Norah and Gabby, and can always be spotted with a novel tucked under her arm. When she is not reading or writing, she can be found dancing, or playing piano while dreaming about books.

Made in the USA
Columbia, SC
27 June 2017